# THE
# MUSTARD SEED
# 2095

John T. Hourihan, Jr.

*Lavender Press*
*Blue Fortune Enterprises, LLC*

*This book is dedicated to Lin, my wife,
who has never let me give up on my work.*

*He said, "How will we liken the Kingdom of God? Or with what parable will we illustrate it? It's like a grain of mustard seed, which, when it is sown in the earth, though it is less than all the seeds that are on the earth, yet when it is sown, grows up, and becomes greater than all the herbs, and puts out great branches, so that the birds of the sky can lodge under its shadow."*

**– Mark 4:30–32, *The Holy Bible, Catholic Edition***

*"In all of us, even in good men, there is a lawless wild-beast nature, which peers out in sleep."*
**– Socrates**

# Prologue

*Four billion years ago, he had looked out with the eagerness of a child over what had been created for him by his elder. The maelstrom of dust and gas, blackness and gravity were all reinvented for him inside his mind, everything that was created from nothing. Violent collisions of matter, light, and fire coalesced into formations. Then the formations began to enlarge, attracting more and more gas and dust into objects. Soon they found their patterns and began to orbit each other on a journey through the universes.*

*"Where were we in this?" he asked his elder.*

*"Not yet," was the only answer. "Watch."*

*The smaller objects began journeys around the larger and intensely heated gas giants. The fire giants spread into the universes and dragged their children with them. Aeons later, the children began to cool, holding the heat from the fire giant deep inside them.*

*Volcanoes on the surfaces of the children, planets, added gases from the still hot interior to the atmosphere. Methane covered the planet. Hydrogen and oxygen added water and the outer surface cooled more.*

*"Where were we?" asked the young one.*

*"We were being created here, just now, in the age of volcanoes from the light given off by the fire giant sun. We were on Earth when the crust began and liquid water formed on the outer surface. We watched the early protozoic life form, and never believed it would come to replace us on Earth, but it is also a curse to live so long." The young one watched as plants brought photosynthesis and the earth greened and the oceans turned blue.*

*"We spirits reigned here alone for billions of years, then we were told to farm the mats of microbes, then the plants, then the beings of matter, and we were told to tend to them all."*

*The elder turned his attention elsewhere and the vision stopped. "You know the end." The vision faded to black and the young one returned to his genetics lessons.*

# Chapter One

*"Let there be among you a person who understands. When the crop ripened, he came quickly carrying a sickle and harvested it. Anyone here with two good ears had better listen!"*
*- The Gospel of Thomas, Nag Hammadi, Codex II*

*"There are three classes of people: those who see. Those who see when they are shown. Those who do not see."*
*- Leonardo da Vinci*

It was warm for June and getting warmer as Campaign Formulator Sixth Level Raphael Aronson, halfway up the outside wrought-iron stairway to his apartment building, paused to let his breath catch up with him. "Jesus," he said. "I don't believe this heat."

He wiped the sweat from his forehead with the back of his right hand and looked out over the hazy cityscape below from the safety of the ninth floor of the Radisson Building.

He lived on the eighteenth floor. His whole body was drenched from the walk home and the climb up the side of the building. With the systematic eradication of the central federal government, beginning in the first few decades of the millennium nearly seventy-five years ago, most people had moved back to the cities. They didn't all fit. It was crowded, but the outlying towns were just too "uncontrolled." This state was one of the ones that had given up and let their police forces go and their infrastructure dissolve. From then on, local boards, dominated by those who could make money, now made the laws. For instance, the small Massachusetts town Raphael had come from as a boy was now being run by the company that owned the water. The company was owned by Tod Berga, who was suspected to be the richest man in the country, if not the world. Raphael Aronson looked down the side of the granite building. He was happy to be here in New Clovis. Life was good.

"It's like a mountain," he thought, "and I live in a cave on the side of it. But with a TV."

Below him, Enterprise Boulevard came to a "T" with Republic Avenue just at the entrance to his building. He never entered the building at the downstairs doorway because the climb inside was stifling compared to being outside in the free air. Well, it was sort of free, Raphael thought. His electric bill had recently added a small charge at the bottom called, "Your fair share for clean air." He thought it ironic that the power companies had done away with all regulations and polluted the air, and they were now charging their customers to cut down on the filth the companies had put in there themselves. "Wouldn't it be nice if they were just better people," he thought.

Enterprise, a street that long ago was the heart of the financial district, was now a mile-long downhill gauntlet of cracked roadway bordered by crumbling sidewalks. Raphael thought that he could remember when automobiles used to fill the street with blaring horns and screeching tires taking the turn too fast and drivers shouting out the opened windows at each other. That was before the decimation of the Middle East by the French and Americans in the third decade of the century turned the only oil fields left into a glowing desert, the sand having turned to glass from the bombs. The government explained to everyone, after the end of the Middle East war, that there was no more oil left for consumers. The Republic compensated everyone for the gas-powered automobiles they turned in and banned the manufacture of new ones. Within a few decades, the population was ready to absorb an all-out ban on driving. The auto manufacturers were soothed with new orders for war vehicles and material. There were new war plants established throughout the country, and it became one's patriotic duty to live near one and work there, so there were plenty of jobs, and people no longer needed to drive long distances to work. It was like beating the plow shares, eighteen-wheelers, and family cars back into weapons.

Now, with all the cars gone, Enterprise was a frighteningly raucous walkway of city people heading to and from work, walking down the center of the road equidistant from the side-dwellers of homeless families in makeshift tents, and black market vendors selling cigarettes, music vids, beer and TV minutes, and the pick pockets and thugs on roller skates or motorized skateboards who, because of the ceaseless boredom, were looking for a chance to change what they did yesterday into something new for today.

There were some one-story century-old houses tucked in between three- and four-story buildings, but most of the zone was full of tents tucked between the buildings. Whenever his walk home from work arrived at Enterprise, Raphael would pull back his un-tucked shirt to expose his .38 revolver. It made the walk home feel safer, even though pretty much everyone else had a weapon too, and the un-policed world lived under the threat of mutually assured individual destruction.

The second law of the New Republic guaranteed that everyone could have a gun. It had been a remnant of an earlier time, like so many of the rules. Of course, also like so many of the rules, the second rule was counter-weighted by the sixth rule, "Thou shalt not kill, except in war."

That is where he was coming from now, work at campaign headquarters. The late afternoon sunlight glinted off the higher windows on the right side of the street. He watched the haze of fog roll up the street from Fisherman's Wharf. No one knew why it was still named after fishermen when there hadn't been any fish in the bay for nearly seventy years. Raphael, now in his mid-thirties, seemed to remember his grandfather fishing at a lake somewhere off in the interior, but that was of course before the purge; before the Republic became the Republic and the environmental laws were discarded as needless and counter-productive, and the earth, especially near the city, became a cesspool surrounded by buildings. It wasn't good for the health of anything except the drain flies, which flourished in the cities.

At the eighteenth floor, he pushed open the door and stepped inside. He always enjoyed the first ten or twelve floors because of the view, but then his fear of heights took over and he clutched with white knuckles the iron rail bolted to the outside stairway for the last six or eight floors. With the height of his anxiety growing with each step, he was always happy and relieved to reach the top and push inside the door to the safety of the hallway to his room and the rooms of six other campaign workers. He never went to the roof as the others did in the evenings. He liked the breeze and the sight of the birds, but the heights were too oppressive. He did his mandatory exercise in his room.

The darkened hall was hot enough, so the Kelly-green walls seemed to be leaning inward. Toward the end, he approached his room: number 418. He adjusted the picture he had thumb-tacked to the center of the door panel just above the number. It was a picture his great-grandfather had kept from the old days when his family owned a farm. It featured a strange horse that Raphael assumed was one of the animals that had been on the farm. The heat and humidity during the summer months caused the cardboard to slip nearly every day, and each evening, he would have to set it straight again. The picture was his small attempt at individuality. He had no idea why he would tempt things that way, but it just felt refreshing to have his door look a little different from the other ones on the floor.

"Similarity breeds contentment." The thought slipped into his mind uninvited.

Inside his room, he headed directly to the "energy saving" window air controller and twisted the knob to the right, trying to coax cooler air from the device. The whir of the quartz-driven motor added itself to the hum from the one attached to the overhead light. He walked to the kitchen table next to the second, and only other, window and sat where he could see Republic Avenue stretch downhill all the way to the airport. He liked to eat his dinner here and watch the camouflaged airplanes arrive and depart to and from the war in the Southwest. It seemed the country had always been at war with Mexico since the wall had been built during the beginning of the twenty-first century.

Before cooking, he decided to watch television. He slid his credit card into the slot at the bottom of his sixty-five-inch Samsung and turned to ESPN6. Six was where his favorite team was broadcast. It was one of the "Entitled" channels. Usually, being a Member, he would watch the On Demand pay channels, but he enjoyed the games nearly as much as the "Entitleds," and tonight the Patriots were playing.

He hurried to the sink to draw water. The electricity would

stay on for the entirety of the game since the electric company was owned by the Republic, but the water usually went off around seven-thirty or eight, and he was going to need enough for dinner, his weekly bath, enough for coffee, and to shave in the morning. A heavy chlorine smell rose from the three buckets he was filling through a short length of hose attached to the kitchen faucet.

It was 6:40. There was still enough time to open a beer and check the numbers for today's lottery before the football game started. Although Raphael enjoyed a level of comfort in the rules of the Republic, he also appreciated many of the things the "Entitleds" were allowed to consume but only in the privacy of his apartment. There was no need to tell anyone else. Just as he returned from his water chores, his microwave dinged, and he pulled his USR-sanctioned dinner out, burned his fingers, and dropped the cardboard tray without spilling the contents onto the counter.

"It is your responsibility," he sing-songed, mimicking the voice in the daily meditations, "to keep yourself healthy by exercise, meditation, and eating the prescribed USR meals five times a week." He usually left his dinner feeling hungry, but hunger was just part of life for all but the Republic and some of the Associates.

He pulled the microwavable cardboard tray of vegetable lasagna from the counter and sat it on the table in front of him. He adjusted his chair with the knob on the bottom so he could see the TV, but since the game hadn't started yet, he absent-mindedly began to read the food box as he ate.

**INGREDIENTS:** veg. lasagna patty (pasta, duram wheat flour, niacin, iron, thiamine mononitrate, riboflavin, folic acid) silicon dioxin, water, eggs, egg whites, whey, milk, cream vinegar, xanathan gum, locust bean gum, guar gum, pinto beans, spinach, cultured milk solids, salt, enzymes…" He would have read the next half of the ingredients, but the game had begun.

As usual, the Patriots, his team, jumped out to an early lead. He seemed to remember hating this team at some time in the past, but it was now somehow satisfying and calming that they nearly always won, and on the very rare occasion when they did lose, the announcers blamed it on the referees, and everyone took solace in hating the officials. He didn't know anyone who wasn't a Patriots fan, so there were very few sports arguments, only the weekly dose of satisfaction with the win. Again, tonight they bested the London Merchantiles, and as he switched off the TV, Raphael heard himself reiterating the team motto, "If you want it, earn it. Do your job." It was also the first rule of the Republic.

He walked his practiced route around the room, shutting off each four-inch disc-shaped quartz generator attached to each appliance in the apartment. Just before he unplugged his wallet from the cable in the wall, he heard the clang of an old cash register as his winnings from the football game were added automatically to his card.

"Save energy or go without," he chimed (Rule 15) when all his devices, except for the TV which he had switched to mute, had been shut down for the night. He laughed. Raphael didn't mind the rules. They just seemed like common sense to him, and they popped into his head at the most appropriate times as reminders. He wondered if others went through the same thing. He was more than content with his profession as a campaign supervisor level six. He loved his job, and as he slid into bed and pulled the covering sheet up over his shoulders, he smiled in anticipation of the morning, his workout, and his walk to work. Life was good for Raphael Aronson. The rules kept people in check even without police, and there was nothing that he couldn't live his way through with a modicum of happiness.

# CHAPTER TWO

*Jesus said, "If your leaders say to you, 'Look, the (Father's)
kingdom is in the sky,' then the birds of the sky will precede you.
If they say to you, 'It is in the sea,' then the fish will precede you.
Rather, the (Father's) kingdom is within you and it is outside
you. When you know yourselves, then you will be known, and you
will understand that you are children of the living Father.
But if you do not know yourselves, then you live in poverty,
and you are the poverty."*

*– The Gospel of Judas Didymos Thomas, third verse,
Nag Hammadi, Codex II*

Seventy-eight degrees was too hot for 5:30 a.m. The sun was already streaming through the windows, as was the smell of someone's breakfast, bacon and eggs, cooking. Raphael sat up at the edge of the bed and reached for the remote. He liked to check the news, sports, and weather first thing every morning. It brightened his day.

"It's going to be a scorcher," the young male announcer said happily. "Blame it on el Nino."

"See that?" Raphael said with a raised eyebrow. "It's not global warming. It's el Nino. We stopped driving cars, and everything went back to normal." He glanced out the window at the red and orange sunrise waking up the city. By the time he was eating his USR bran muffin and pouring his fair-trade coffee, the news and highlights of the Patriot win had gone by, and the woman announcer was telling the news of the war in Africa.

"Now, teamed with Russia and Iceland, our USR troops on the Second Front have swarmed through Chad and Niger with little loss of lives, but several dozen drones have been destroyed by our enemy, so high five to our boys and girls. The cost of the war has reached $1.6 trillion a month. The Dow jumped 300 points at closing yesterday and is expected to jump again this morning. Remember Rule Six, 'Thou shalt not kill, except in war.' Respect the draft. Back to you, Elmond."

She smiled and held up her hand to the TV audience for them to reciprocate the gesture. Raphael high-fived the air with his right hand as he snatched his .38 from the bedside table drawer and slid it into the holster at his waist with the left. He was content in the belief that most of the people who were drafted were Entitleds, not Members such as himself. Checking the apartment from the doorway one last time, he spun and backed out, locked it, and headed down the hall to the outside staircase. Maybe he would be able to retire at seventy-five after all.

Raphael enjoyed the faces of the people he passed on his way to work. There was a practiced disinterest in most of them as they tried, as best they could, to become a victimless part of the crowd, each clinging to his or her personal protection and walking straight ahead. Raphael liked to look directly at their eyes as he passed them. He liked people. Few ever looked back at him, and if they did, it was a quick glance, a mistake of outward connectivity, and then back to the forge-ahead focus.

But then she walked by, headed in the opposite direction, and she looked directly, and without wavering, into his eyes. She smiled, just a hint, but it was enough to make him turn as he passed. Her expression almost dragged a reciprocal smile from Raphael. Then he turned back toward the Campaign Headquarters two miles farther down Enterprise and quickened his pace. He glanced over his shoulder, but all he could see was her striding away. Her red hair reached to the small of her back and swayed with her brisk and carefree step. Below the red hair was a pair of the shortest white shorts Raphael had ever seen. They made him smile too.

Before he could forget her, he had arrived at his job. He worked at the one business that had no off season: political elections. He pushed through the revolving doors and went straight for the staircase. When he arrived at the sixth floor, he pushed open the door and headed for the coffee room.

"Good morning, Raphael. Great game last night, huh?"

Morgan Baez was a seventh level and Raphael's supervisor. She was a tall, well-kept, and extremely competent woman in her mid to late forties. Her bright blue contact lenses were appropriate for her shoulder-length hair, which was now blonde and pulled into a bun. She had a roundish but not fat face, and her figure was heavier than it had been when he first met her fifteen years ago, but she was still very obviously female. Once, Raphael had even had a fleeting daydream of what might happen if they ever got together, and it was not an unpleasant fantasy. It was easy to have Morgan Baez for a boss. Everyone respected her.

"Again," he answered.

"Today's the day."

"I'm ready," Raphael answered. "When's the meeting? Ten?"

"Right, ten sounds good. See you then."

They went in opposite directions as she strode to her office on the seventh floor and he continued to the coffee room.

"Hey, Raphael." Dylan Stofe greeted him as he entered the coffee room.

Raphael didn't like Dylan. Dylan was one of the photosyzers. It was Dylan's job to alter the reality of a photograph of a candidate so it would look more like what the campaign wanted to portray, while maintaining as much of the real person as possible: a blurring of the mole on a cheek, a hair trim, reduction of a few pounds, whiter teeth, tightening of the skin in key areas. Raphael, for his part, worked portraying a perfect candidate by assessing what the voters wanted and then creating an entire reality that coincided with the perception. Only then a live person would be chosen to fill the characterization. It wasn't the differences between his job and Stofe's job that bothered Raphael. It was more the similarities, the looking into the mirror that caused the irritation.

"Dylan, how's it going?"

"Well, you know, livin' the dream. The Re-pubic is exceptional."

Dylan finished pouring his coffee, took two packets of black-market sugar and an envelope of creamer from his pocket, dumped them into his cup and left the room, headed for his cubicle. He stopped and turned. "Hey, I have a few homemade scones at my desk if you want one."

"No, but thanks." Raphael was more partial to the USR boxed donuts delivered once a week to his apartment. He also never liked how Dylan and a few of his friends made light of the rules of the Republic. This one he had just slighted had been number eight: "I believe in the goodness of the Republic because the Republic is exceptional."

There were those who hated the Republic and its rules. There were even rumors of some kind of overthrow that was being planned; if so, he thought Dylan Stofe would be a likely candidate.

Raphael didn't remember when he had first learned the rules, but he assumed it was probably during his childhood. The rules had always worked well for him, and people who made fun of them irritated him almost to his bones. He never really understood why it seemed to grate at his nerves the way it did, but he just accepted that it did. He had an inborn loyalty to the authority that kept his life stable.

He took his black coffee to his desk and pulled up his newest character assessment on the computer. He would present it today to the delegation assigned to choose a candidate within the next few weeks. He read his assessment on the screen. "Forty-five years old, six foot two, athletic build, blond hair, brown eyes, tan skin to the point of racial ambiguity, Christian church-goer, worked his way up through the Health and Disaster Agency, born in New Boston, decorated veteran of the Mexican wars, adept at basketball, a hunter who eats anything he kills, a man with calluses on his hands from hard work in the past but who has amassed a fortune through greed and ingenuity. He is married to a quiet but lovely Asian woman; both have sex partners on the side, the son of a high-ranking military man and his diplomat wife, a staunch conservative, two children—a boy and a girl. His motto is…"

After months of research through polls and current trends, it was the last thing needed for his presentation, a motto worthy of the next man to be elected. No one knew when that would be or for what office, but it was policy to have the next to run for office in the can and ready for dissemination.

"His motto is…" Raphael stared at the screen and let his mind go blank. This worked for him often. If he concentrated on nothing, the words would come to him. He smiled. "That's it. His motto is 'If you want it, work for it. Do your job.'"

Carrying his coffee and a printout of the biography and other background of his political fable, he climbed the stairs to the seventh floor. When he reached the door to the conference room, Dylan stepped in front of him and opened the door for him, carrying his own bundle of papers. They sat across from each other at the center of the rectangular table, arranged their work in front of themselves, and waited in awkward silence.

Next into the conference room was thirteen-year-old, newly hired Trudy Green, a political analyst who was the newest perfect face and tight body hired by Morgan Baez. Before she even got a chance to sit down, Morgan entered and was closely followed by Carleen Dumas, the Casting Director who would be charged with putting the work of all the others together and finding a human being to fit the mold.

The work would have been much more intriguing if it wasn't so constant. There was always an election to fill, always a new profile to create, a new human to find, a new Frankenstein's monster to run out in front of the "Entitleds" for their voting approval. It was never a chore getting your person elected if you did your job right. The Entitleds were the most populous of the citizens by far, so they pretty much elected everyone if they could be cajoled to vote, but they were easy to judge. They mostly wanted to not be bothered by facts or policies. They coveted their simple lives of daily work, nightly relaxation, two-week vacation, an ample beer ration, plenty of TV minutes on their cards, every kind of sex possible, and every once in a while, when it was necessary, the Republic would call on the patriotism of the Entitleds to subdue, oppress, or outright get rid of a politician or, for that matter, any person who went wrong, or to shout down a group of people who wanted more than was being offered. Raphael knew that all he had to do was trot out in front of them the person they believed they were, even though there was no similarity whatsoever, and they would vote for him. He also knew what the Entitleds should have known, that if the Republic got more, everyone else would have more. It was just the way things worked.

"Are we waiting for Barry?" Morgan directed her question to everyone in the room.

The Barry she was asking about was Barry Gold. If Raphael had a friend other than Morgan, it was Barry Gold, the well-established Media Controller of the Campaign Division of the Republic.

Raphael answered, "I don't think we need a controller yet. Nothing is public."

"Okay then, let's get started. Questions?"

"Why forty-five-years old?" Trudy the analyst asked even before anyone else was finished reading the copies Raphael had dealt to each.

"Old enough to be respected but still young enough to be sexual." He thought he saw Trudy blush but dismissed it as a result of the heat in the room, even with the windows open. Everyone nodded their acceptance of Raphael's answer.

"How can he be racially ambiguous and have blond hair?" Will Worton, the fact creator asked, seemingly to Raphael, for no apparent reason except to be included in the conversation. Raphael looked at him with a stare just a little short of disdain. "Okay, so he has brown hair. Hair color is not a big deal, as long as it isn't pink like some of the Entitleds."

"And why is this not a woman?" Still Worton.

"Because it was a woman last time. We have to balance out the genetic makeup or we start getting idiot children, like you." It barely made even metaphorical sense, but no one liked Will, so it sufficed. There was a nervous laugh around the table, but Raphael received a stern look from Morgan. Among the people Raphael had no respect for were Dylan Stofe and Will Worton. They seemed to him to have no idea why they were at the campaign building or what their purpose was. Raphael thought they acted more like Entitleds with a job rather than Members with a profession.

Carleen, the campaign formulator, spoke next. "Raphael, could it be somewhere other than New Boston? You know a lot of the country doesn't like those intellectuals from up there. Actually, the Republic frowns on intellectuals, elites, academics, and free thinkers altogether, and the Entitleds just out-and-out hate them."

"I thought of that, but it is also where the Patriots are from, and a lot of Entitleds love their football team."

"Remember when everyone hated these guys?" Dylan asked and gave a short laugh. "Seems like, what, a year or two ago, and now they're the only team worth watching. Boy, tell an Entitled how you don't like the Pats and you are definitely going to lose some teeth."

"Or get shot," Worton added.

"Okay." Raphael nodded in agreement. "We can have him come from somewhere else, but where do you want the guy to be from?"

"I don't know. Maybe mid-country? Not from the Southwest. You have him racially ambiguous, and some might equate that with Mexicans. I don't think we need the Mexican vote, do you?"

"Okay, how about the Iowa wasteland? They don't even have a football team, and no one knows where it is or what the people stand for past being white, carnivorous, and Christian evangelical."

"Okay, fat, white, Bible thumpers it is. The rest of this is fine." Morgan looked to her casting supervisor. "Is this doable, Carleen?"

"Sure. I already have someone in mind if I can get him married to an Asian woman. What's the post?"

"Don't know yet," Morgan returned, "but we are due for a new Secretary of Food and Water, so… maybe we won't even have to worry about votes."

She moved some papers and looked down at her appointment book. "Let's get started, and see you all Friday?" After a pause, she added, "Raphael, hang around a second. I need to run something by you. And Carleen?" Carleen stopped at the door and turned back. "Carleen, make sure he's a Member, and could you come back in, say, fifteen minutes?

My computer is acting up again. I think it's a virus of some sort."

"Member, okay, that goes without saying. See you in fifteen," Carleen answered and left.

The others followed, and when the door closed behind them, Morgan asked, "Do you feel like putting together a presidential characterization?"

"Sure." Raphael was tired of local and statewide creations and cabinet posts. It had been seven years since he had put together the presidential outline that had produced the runner-up in the last election. He had wondered if he would get the chance again this time. It wasn't his fault that the guy Carleen picked had been killed in a bar brawl in the Entitleds zone.

"Hope it turns out better than last time," he said to his friend.

"Sure," said Morgan. "Hope this one makes it to the election alive. I still say we could have popped someone else into your characterization and no one would even have known the difference." She paused. "Hey, what did you think of that meditation this morning?"

"Don't know. I had a bath this morning and didn't get a chance to meditate. Why?"

"I don't know. It was just a little weird."

Not knowing what to say, Raphael nodded his dismissal and started for the door.

"Do you think Trudy is too young?"

He didn't like being asked his personal opinion on things, but his friend Morgan was also his boss, and he figured this could be a test.

"I don't think so. A lot of the analysts are young. I mean, Trudy has, what, four years' experience at, where did she work?"

"I know, but…" Morgan lined up her papers, placed them on the table, and looked at Raphael. "I know that, but what do you think, personally? You know what I mean."

"Well, in the 30s when it was found out that three-quarters of the people on social welfare were children, the Republic solved it by giving them Rule 12."

"I know Rule 12. 'Children should not be forced into school and hunger but should be afforded the right to work'. I am well aware of it." She paused. "But that's not what I meant, and you know it."

Raphael grabbed his papers and his coffee and turned toward the door of the conference room with his back to his not slightly promiscuous friend. "She's too young, Morgan." He paused. "And you know it, or you wouldn't have asked."

He left the room, letting the door close softly with a click.

## CHAPTER THREE

The phone on his kitchen wall rang while he was pulling on his clothes. It was Friday, his final day to hear about how far the new characterization had come and what each member of the team had done with the initial outline. The position had indeed been for the Secretary of Food and Water. As he crossed the living room, he reached down, grabbed the remote, and turned down the meditation he had been listening to, proceeded to the kitchen, and answered the phone. His mother had once told him that, in the past, telephones had been cellular, and you could carry them with you wherever you went, but once China had established that it was capable of shooting down satellites, the world followed course, and soon only the weather and military and a few communications satellites were left. No country wanted to start a cascading practice of shooting down the military and weather types, he had been told. It helped that growing interference with the reception of the cell phones ate away at the quality of any handheld communication device. It was followed by a rebirth of land lines, and as quickly as the mobile-phone fad had begun, it ended. People accepted the demise readily because it added jobs refurbishing the underground telephone lines across the world. Everyone was happy.

"Hey Raphael." It was Barry Gold.

"Hi, what's going on?"

"I got a date."

"That's nice. Is she alive and fully sighted? Any obvious evidence of recessive genes in the pool?"

"Funny. Look, she wants me to double up, you know, get a friend."

"I don't think so. When?"

"Tonight."

"I don't know. Maybe. I don't know who I could get to go out on such short notice."

"How about the analyst?"

"Are you nuts? Trudy? She's like thirteen years old."

"No one with that set of knockers is thirteen years old. And those eyes, and that…"

"Enough," Raphael cut in. "You're making me nauseous. She's a child."

"Yeah well, childhood ain't what it used to be since Bovine Growth Hormone. We pump the cows full of it and then the kids drink the milk and, voila, womanhood. And then there's the estrogen in the drinking water." Gold was referring to the unexpected side effect of birth control pills that found their way straight through the body and into treatment plants, and through the treatment plants back into the water beginning in the twentieth century, and now most potable water was inundated with estrogen, and most of the men Raphael knew were an almost even balance between male and female. This was not the case with his friend Barry or himself. Neither drank much water.

"You know what? I'll call you later this afternoon. Maybe."

"Find someone or ask the kid. She'll say yes. I bet you a hundred bucks."

"Tempting, but no. I'm still a Christian. Talk to you later."

"Hey, did you do the meditation today?"

"Up until you called. Why?" Raphael was lying. He was supposed to sit down and listen to the meditations, but lately he hadn't been.

"Wasn't it weird about the football thing? The last rule, Rule 20, finished the first part of the meditation with 'inebriate, fornicate, proliferate,' as usual, but then added 'Go Patriots!'"

"I was making breakfast at the same time. Did it really say Go Patriots?"

"Yup. Strange huh? Hey, how long ago was it that we all hated these guys?"

"I don't know. Seems like a lifetime, though. Well, talk to you later."

Raphael hung up the phone and looked back toward the

silent TV that was still broadcasting the picture of the end of the meditation. He walked back into the living room and turned it back up. The woman announcer was finishing up.

"And that is the meditation for today. Namaste. And now back to the news."

A blond male announcer with an obviously unnecessary stylish comb-over chimed in, "The war in Africa has been going well, about as well as can be expected. Chad, Niger, Libya, Egypt, and Sudan have all been liberated, and not without incredible losses in ammunition, supplies, and equipment. The war in the Southwest against Mexico has stalled in mid-Arizona. The effect on the DOW has been appropriate, up another 270 points yesterday. Hold on to those 401Ks people. They will be going up soon. What a great war, right Charlize?"

Raphael clicked off the TV. He had been shaving off twelve percent of his paycheck every month and had been funneling it into his 401K retirement account since he began working at nine years old. Back then, he was a courier for the department he still worked in. He expected to retire as soon as he could, seventy-five was his goal, but once he retired, he would no longer be considered a full Member, and he would have to pay for his apartment rent, his food, his health care, water, sewer, electricity. The only things that would still be free would be his phone and his TV. It seemed to him that when you reached an age when the money being spent on you was more than what you were pumping into the government by way of the heavy taxes on the Members and Entitleds who worked, and by the tithes meted out by the churches who were now part of the government, nobody cared if you lived or died any longer. It was that time that you had to anticipate, because if you owned anything, people would be coming for it.

He took a quick look in the full-length mirror on the back of his bathroom door to see if he was presentable for work, and then stopped. He looked a little more intensely at the thirty-six-year-old who stared back and wondered if a thirteen-year-old such as Trudy might actually be interested in him at all. His hair was short and a healthy looking dark brown, and he had a nice tan from his everyday walks. His face was still unwrinkled and clean shaven except for short sideburns. He had nice brown eyes and was in good shape from not fudging on his exercises, and he made a judgment. "Not bad," he said and left the room.

As he climbed down the building and into the street, he turned in anticipation that he would see the redhead again. It wasn't long before his prayer was answered. He picked her out of the crowd while she was still nearly fifty yards in front of him, her red hair bobbing in the sea of workers. As she got closer, he wondered if he should speak to her. But what should he say? Should he ask her to go with him tonight? Before he could make a decision, she was five yards in front of him, looking directly at him as if she too had been anticipating the meeting.

Suddenly she stopped and smiled broadly at him as if they knew each other. She was beautiful, with impeccably tanned skin, brown eyes bordering on black, and magnetic dark lips. He stopped too and drank in her body that was covered only with a purple halter top with a plunging neckline and the same white shorts. Around her neck was a dainty gold chain, and from it hung two pendants, one a fleur-de-lis, the other a golden bee with red glass inserts in the wings. He started to speak, "I'm sorry do I know…" but before he could finish his sentence, she smiled and began walking again. He spent the rest of the walk to the campaign HQ feeling foolish and childish. But not for long.

As he was pouring his coffee in the break room, he felt a presence behind him. He casually turned his head to see who else might be in the room with him and realized it was Trudy. Gold's comment drew Raphael's eye directly to her chest. His friend had been right. Her white see-through blouse was opened a few buttons from the top, but it didn't matter. He could see everything right through the sheer material, and she was wearing nothing else under it. He forced himself to look at her face and realized she was even more beautiful than the girl he had seen on the street.

"Hi Mr. Aronson," she said, with an unwavering stare into his eyes.

"Trudy." He returned his attention to the counter in front of him, pouring almond milk into the cup of dark coffee.

"I have a question for you," she said and stepped away from the door and toward him.

He turned, and this time managed to look at her face. She

looked so young to have that body.

"Do you think this blouse shows too much? I mean, we are supposed to be sexual in the office place, right?"

He choked just a bit and tried to manage a response that would be appropriate. He felt it really was too much but didn't want to hurt her feelings or make himself out to be either a prude or a lecher.

"Because Mr. Worton told me I should go home and change."

He found the words. "Maybe Mr. Worton is the one who has to change. You look wonderful. Go back to work."

She smiled and leaned against the door jamb as he walked by. "Thanks," she said and turned just a bit to let him brush up against her as he passed. By the time Raphael got to his cubicle, he had to sit down.

"Damn," he said to himself, but he spoke the words out loud, and Morgan, who was now standing beside him, answered.

"She looks pretty good today, doesn't she? Don't forget what you told me. You know what's true for the goose is true for the gander."

He laughed a little, allowing his friend to be right. "I never thought of you as a goose," he said.

"Well, it's Friday. Today is the day for the final. See you later?"

"Yup, I'm ready... Hey Morgan, are you doing anything tonight?"

Baez took a short breath. *What the hell is he doing*, she

thought. *Is he going to ask me out?*

"Not really. Why?"

"Gold needs someone to double with him because his first-dater wants some company, I guess. We could go, have a nice dinner. What do you think?"

She stopped for a few seconds, confused. "Well sure, why not? When?"

"Not sure. I'll let you know when Gold gets in."

The day proceeded like every other Friday. Gold came to work late and obviously a little worse for the wear of last night, and a time was set up for them to all meet in front of Le Renard restaurant, on the edge of the Entitleds zone near the airport.

At the meeting, Carleen Dumas introduced the candidate she had chosen to fit the information she had been given at mid-week. His name was Merl Bridges, and this morning he fit everything down to the letter. "Can we set up some shots today?" Dylan said. "I'd kind of like to get going. Now that we know what the post is, we don't have much time left before the installment."

"Do we know who he is running against?" Worton asked.

"No one," Trudy admonished sharply. "It's an appointment."

There were a few muffled laughs at Worton's embarrassment at being shot down by a thirteen-year-old.

"Oh, and by the way Mr. Worton." *Oh Jesus, here it comes,* thought Raphael. "Mr. Aronson thinks maybe you ought to be the one to change, not me." (She was playing with him, with both of them.)

"He would," Worton scowled. "The blouse is… I was just trying to… oh the hell with it. Come to work naked for all I care."

As Raphael juggled whether or not he should say anything at all, Barry Gold slapped him on the back and laughed, and Morgan shook her head. The meeting was dismissed.

Sexual tension at work had become a given over the years. The Entitleds even took it a step further in that they felt it was their duty to bed as many people as possible and perform as many sexual practices on them as long as they were of the opposite sex, and if they weren't, oh well. One cult had even taken Rule 20 as a basis for their religion. Raphael thought it might have been a side effect, but he was under the impression that could have just been an excuse to have indiscriminate sex. Sex being the real opium of the people in 2095 in New Clovis and most other cities worldwide.

# Chapter Four

*"Rather the kind of existence they had was like that of a seed, or it may be compared with that of an embryo. He had made them in the manner of the word, which exists in a seminal state before the things it will bring forth have yet come into being."*
*- The Gospel of Truth, Nag Hammadi scriptures, Codex I*

Raphael stood in the bathroom and shaved for the second time that day. The TV blared so he could hear it from the next room. He was getting ready for his date with Morgan. He bathed and shaved and used some of his Christmas present from the office, a large bottle of 4711, a smell-good tonic for everyone regardless of gender. He had turned the volume up because he wanted to hear the new meditation everyone had been discussing. From time to time, he peered into the living room from the bathroom to see what was being broadcast. It was the ocean. He always loved this one since he had never seen the ocean for real. He had seen the bay, but that was so disgusting he tried to avoid it whenever he could, and it couldn't really pass for what he now saw on the screen.

The expanse of pristine water on the TV met an almost identically colored sky, and the soft waves lapped the sand in the forefront. "The Republic is from the ocean," a calm woman's voice monotoned. "The Republic will return to the ocean. The ocean is calm and deep. Feel the ebb and flow. Breathe in the salt air, the smell of the incensed perfume of the yellow elders. Taste the red fruit and feel the pleasant sting of the north breeze. Breathe in, hold it, breathe out, relax all your muscles, and hear the rules one more time.

"Listen to the Mandate of the Republic:

1. Do your job. If you want it, earn it.

2. The right of the people to be armed shall not be infringed.

3. The more the Republic has, the more will be returned to the Entitled.

4. Pledge allegiance to the flag of the Republic.

5. The Republic is one nation under the Christian god.

6. Thou shalt not kill, except in war.

7. It is the responsibility of the Members to stay healthy by exercising, meditating, and eating the correct USR foods.

8. Believe in the goodness of the Republic because the Republic is exceptional.

9. Similarity breeds contentment. Work for the good of all.

10. The government must remain small and be ruled by

we the Republic.

11. Sexual desire is a God given right.

12. We must have a strong military, so respect the draft.

13. Children should not be forced into schools or hunger but should be afforded the right to work.

14. Save energy or go without.

15. Your prayers will be answered.

16. All those entitled to vote shall be cared for by the Republic.

17. A crime against one is a crime against all.

18. The Republic, be she right or wrong, she is always my Republic.

19. There is no need to steal. We each have enough.

20. Inebriate, fornicate, proliferate. Go Patriots.”

Raphael's eyes snapped wide, and he nicked himself with the razor.

“What?”

No wonder everyone loved the football team. It seemed he had never heard anything like this before. It seemed to him the rules had always ended with the word “proliferate.”

He stepped into the living room and saw that the ocean motif was gone and that the symbol of the football team was emblazoned on the screen, a red, white, and blue caricature of an American Revolutionary soldier from the eighteenth century. He laughed out loud, as he switched the TV to “mute.” In order to save energy, the TVs were supposed to be always left on. Morgan had explained to him once that to turn on the television took more power than to leave it on. It didn't make much sense, but it didn't bother him enough to care. Most often he used the mute button. Rules were rules.

He trundled down the stairs to street level, stepped off the fire escape, and proceeded into the asphalt street. It was wet from a short afternoon rain, and it reflected light from the sides. It was as shiny as ice in darkness but not slippery.

As Raphael walked down the center of the street, he could see, in the distance at the bottom of the hill, the demarcation of the end of the Members' zone and the beginning of the villages where the Entitleds lived. Up until the zone change, the lights had been more purposeful; a muted green restaurant sign, a blue-light-lined shop called The Zodiac, a white-lit jewelry store, but at the crossroad at the bottom of the hill it all changed. The Entitled section looked as if Christmas had just exploded in red, green, orange, blue, purple, and white lights. The heavy smell of outdoor-cooking meat floated in waves through the air, and a crushing feeling of uncertainty made Raphael unbutton his coat and show his .38.

He was to meet Morgan at the edge of the French quarter, and then they would walk together to the airport road where there was a short string of fine restaurants before the heart of the gaudy and raucous zone where the Entitleds lived. Gold and his date would meet them there, "In front of Le Renard." The upscale French restaurant was frequented by the Associates, a group of upper-level management who lived among the

Members but discoursed directly with the Republic.

Then suddenly Morgan was standing only a handful of yards in front of him. She looked almost regal, and Raphael was a bit taken with her as he walked toward her through the crowd. He first saw her shining blonde hair. At work, she always had it pulled back tightly into a French twist. Tonight, it fell freely to her shoulders and blew in the slight warm breeze. Her artificially blue eyes were bright, and the multi-colors of the street glowed in them. Then, as he got close enough to see more than her head and bare shoulders, he caught his breath. They had been out before at conferences and the like, but she had always worn her business clothes on these occasions. Tonight was different. She wore a royal blue skintight dress with a neckline that stylishly plunged to her waist, and its length only reached to a midway point between her knees and the top of her legs, and it was so tight it hardly allowed her to walk. As they met on the sidewalk amidst the crowd, Raphael stopped at arms' length, assessed her and said, "Wow, all this just for me?"

"We'll see," Morgan teased, and they continued side-by-each toward Le Renard.

The two had been friends for as long as they had worked together, and that was headed toward a third decade. They had gone out together many times but had never become intimate. Raphael and Morgan were friends in the true sense, and although he knew of her avid sexuality, he never even thought of trying to become part of it, except for that once. As they walked, they held hands, more like family than lovers.

This part of town was the few blocks between the austerity of theaters and the high-class restaurants and shoppes of the Members and Associates and the loud, playful "adult" clubs, street vendors, liquor and lottery shops, sports bars, and the brothels of the Entitleds. Here in the middle was a mix, and at the edge of the mix was the restaurant that the upper class called Le Renard and the Entitleds called The Fox.

There were three "types" of people in Raphael's world. There were the elites, who worked directly for the Republic, the world rulers. They were called the *Associates*. They seemed to be born knowing their lofty place in life. The next step down were those who worked with the Associates but didn't fully know the reality of their own lives. They could be taught what was inbred in the Associates. They were called the Members. And finally, there were the Entitleds. They worked for themselves. They had no idea what was happening in their own world past physical gratification. They were pawns who did not have a vision for their future.

Raphael saw Gold waiting for them anxiously outside the front door. Barry Gold was also in his mid-thirties; he had flowing blond hair much too long for his station in life. It was to his shoulders, more like the length of the Entitleds than a high-level Member. Member men were expected to wear their hair short. Morgan thought he would have been more handsome if his nose hadn't been broken in a fight as a kid. He was an inch or two taller than Raphael, probably six feet, but without having done much in the way of exercise for many years, he was not in very good shape. As they approached, Morgan gave him a playful punch to the stomach and said, "You should be spending more time with me up on the roof at lunch time."

Morgan was famous for her six-minute miles, running around the rooftop of the Campaign Building during lunch.

"Sure," Gold answered. "Maybe we could find some exercise to do other than running."

"You'll have to show up to find out," Morgan teased, and walked past them toward the restaurant, showing off her body.

"Wait, you haven't met my date," Barry Gold interjected, holding his hand out to a girl who had been reading the menu on the door. When she turned, Raphael had reached out his hand to shake before he realized who it was. She smiled and brushed back her red hair. She shook his hand. It was the girl he had seen two days in a row.

"I know you," she said.

Raphael could only nod. She seemed younger than he had initially thought. She appeared to be in her early twenties. Her skin was tighter and softer looking than most of the people living in these streets among the migrant clouds of war-smoke that were so prevalent they circled the globe. Morgan was not lost in the introduction. She reached out and took the girl's hand, softly holding it and looking into her eyes. She shook the hand gently and smiled at her. "Well, you're just plain delicious, aren't you?" She turned to her co-worker Gold and added, "I'm impressed. How did you get her to go out with you?"

She returned her attention to the girl. "My name is Morgan Baez, and you are?"

"Tafari Alexandria Phoenix." It seemed to Raphael that the girl was proud of the name. Raphael figured she had most likely given herself the name.

"So Tafari Alexandria," Morgan said. "I think you are probably in charge here. Are we eating at Le Renard?"

The girl looked from one face to the next. "Are you up for something new?"

"Always," Morgan answered and put her arm around Gold's date.

"It's just a short walk," Tafari said, looked back at the two men who now stood together, smiled, and walked off arm-in-arm with Morgan.

"Lead the way," Raphael agreed, and the four walked toward the Entitled's zone. As they entered the cacophony of light and noise, a nearly naked man with long black hair, wearing only a blue loin cloth, red suspenders, a white derby hat, and a black mask stepped to the edge of the shadows and whispered something to Morgan. She smiled and gently said, "Not tonight." He returned her smile and retreated to the shadowy alleyway beside a bar called The My Kim.

"It's right up here," Tafari said and quickened her step, stopping in front of a sandwich stand the size of a kitchen table. For the first time since they had begun walking, Raphael stepped up beside Morgan, and Gold took Tafari's hand.

"What is this?" Raphael asked.

"It's a French-Indochina sandwich truck," Tafari answered and stepped back so the others could absorb the beauty.

There were four red and gold wooden wheels with thick black rubber bands glued around the outsides of the wheels like tires; two large back wheels about waist high and the two five- or six-inch forward wheels. They carried a metal cart, four feet by six feet and three feet deep. It was painted with a green and red shore next to a blue ocean. The top of the cart was a box the same size as the bottom but was made of clear plastic. Inside the top was an amber light bulb. Below the light and to the left was a pile of perfectly browned French loaves. The bread sat on a shelf next to a grill. The painting on the bottom of the cart was a scene of boats docking on a beach that was engulfed in flames. Sailors with long black hair stood next to the boats on the shore and assessed what appeared to be the inhabitants of the land. Raphael looked away from the painting as a young man approached from the doorway of a soup restaurant and traded glances with Tafari.

"Muon gì?" he asked pleasantly as if she had been here before, often.

"Bon con chuot bánh mì," answered the red-headed girl.

"What language are you speaking?" Gold asked in total surprise.

"Vietnamese," she answered. "This is a Vietnamese sandwich truck. Weren't you listening? It is the best food this side of the, well, this side of anything. Wait until you taste it."

The young man looked at the three who were obviously here for the first time and asked, "Ho có hieu không?" He was wondering if they had understood her order.

"Không," Tafari answered, shaking her head from side to side.

They shared a smile.

The sandwiches were prepared with foot-long soft loaves, *like large hot dog buns*, Raphael thought, and they were filled with peppers and onions cooked in oil with a light fishy tasting sauce and grilled meat sliced in quarter inch by two-inch strips. The sandwiches were filled to overflowing and topped with red pepper and sea salt.

The three followed Tafari into the darkened alley next to the restaurant, where there were a few outdoor tables with strings of subdued multi-colored Christmas lights hanging from around the edge of an umbrella canopy. Christmas seemed to be a constant celebration in the Entitleds zone, but they called it Saturnalia. The four accepted complementary bottles of Vietnamese Bia Larue to drink. Raphael figured it was because they had overpaid for the sandwiches. Then, after about fifteen minutes of silence, while they ate and watched the living theater in the street before them, without any fanfare, Morgan stood and motioned to the Vietnamese vendor, "Xin anh, mot lan nua."

"What the hell? What did you say? You speak it too?" Gold blurted.

"I asked for another one. They are great, aren't they?"

Raphael smiled at his friend's competence, but he wished she hadn't done this in public. It was only here in this zone that other languages were spoken. It was against some unwritten rule to speak anything but English in business. Tafari sat lower in her chair and ducked her head like a child who had been caught doing something naughty.

"By the way, boys," Morgan said over her shoulder as she waited for her food, "you are eating rat sandwiches." She smiled at Tafari.

There were a few glances that were followed by smiling shrugs, and no one left a bite.

"So, what will we do now?" Gold asked as he finished his beer.

"Let's go to my house," Tafari suggested. She waited in her seat, looking inquiringly around the table.

"How far is it?" Raphael asked, calculating that it might be a long walk from the center of the Entitleds zone to any of the apartments in the Members' area.

"I live right back here," she said, pointing a thumb further down the alleyway.

"You live here?" Gold asked. "In this zone?"

She nodded with a smile. "I like it here. Come on."

"Are you Entitled?" Gold asked. Raphael knew that his friend had dated many Entitled girls, had no concerns with it, but neither he nor Gold expected that she was one of them. She didn't have multi-colored hair, extra metal rings in her face and ears, or intricate multi-colored tattoos. She didn't have the bright lipstick or the rainbow of contact lenses that predominated in Entitled girls.

"No, I'm not," Tafari Alexandria answered. She pursed her lips, and Raphael supposed she might be hurt. She rose from her chair and motioned for the others to follow as she strode into the darkness of the alley. She had gone only a handful of yards into the darkness when she opened her door and yellow light flooded out from her home. Morgan followed her inside, trailed by Barry Gold. As Raphael stepped inside the front door, the warmth of the room engulfed him.

"Damn," he said, "There is more color in this room than I have seen since Gold brought that piñata to work for Trudy's birthday."

"I like color," Tafari said as she hustled around the room, rearranging pillows from the couches to the floor. "I usually sit on the floor when it's not raining," she said and smiled.

Raphael now noticed sandbags piled three high and three wide around the inside of the walls to keep the sometimes-flooded streets from getting in. The apartment was in its entirety three rooms: the bedroom, bathroom, and the kitchen/dining/ living room. There was a three-foot-high refrigerator in one corner, hand painted with a similar scene to the one on the sandwich cart. Next to it, a small kitchen table fit snugly against the far wall. A foot-wide shelf encompassed the entire room a few feet above the floor and was adorned with multi-colored candles every few feet. As Tafari quickly circumnavigated the room lighting candles, the others found a comfortable place on the floor full of embroidered or patchwork pillows.

"She lives here," Gold said in the middle of a laugh while the girl was still out of voice range. The others smiled too. Raphael had never known anyone who would opt for the rented apartments of the Entitleds zone when the apartments offered to the Members and Associates were free until the occupants retired and were no longer considered productive. Tafari came back to the circle of friends with a candle for the center of the room and within minutes, she had placed a pitcher of pineapple juice, four glasses, and a bottle of Absinthe in the center.

"So, tell us about this beautiful name," Raphael said.

She shot him a smiling glance. "Well, Tafari is African. It means first-born daughter. My mother named me that."

"And Alexandria?"

"It is French. It means 'defender of mankind'. My father gave it to me. I picked Phoenix myself. It's Egyptian." As she was still speaking, she sat down next to Morgan. Gold changed his seat and plopped beside her, wrapping his arms around her and pulling her close.

"Hey, take it easy. What are you, a Neanderthal?"

"I don't know. What are you, a lesbian?"

"Sometimes," she said demurely, smiling at Morgan, "but not tonight." Turning to Gold, she added, "It's a beautiful island, you know, Lesbos. It is covered with flowers and olive trees and there is an amazing tropical forest on the northwest part of the island. It's one of the most enchanting parts of Greece."

She kissed Gold, then slid toward the center and began pouring drinks. "Did you know this stuff is a hundred-and-seventy-nine proof and is probably the only thing on the planet that doesn't have silicon dioxide in it?" Tafari said as she began distributing drinks to her guests.

"What are you talking about?" Gold asked.

"Haven't you ever looked at the ingredients on the package of what you eat and drink?"

"No," Gold said. "Why would I care?"

"Well, maybe you wouldn't so eagerly eat a rat sandwich if you did," Morgan said.

"I have," Raphael added. "And yes, I've seen silicon dioxide in almost everything. It's even in the USR lasagna," he said, laughing.

"Did you know that when silicon dioxide is compressed or bent, even by vibrations, it gives off an electric charge? Now why would human beings need an electrical charge?" she asked playfully.

Morgan broke in. "Can we get a look at the weather channel for a few minutes? I heard there was supposed to be another big storm tonight, with eighty-mile-an-hour winds. Just want to check."

Tafari switched the TV to the weather channel and turned up the volume. The four watched intently. Morgan was right—the next storm was forecast to hit the city around midnight and looked like it would be fierce, as always.

"El Nino my ass," Gold blurted. "We had these damn

storms last year, too."

"So, we have hours. It's barely seven," Tafari said and clicked off the TV. The three looked at each other in surprise.

"Anyway," she continued, "I've been told that the silicon dioxide is put into our food on purpose."

"That's a bit paranoid, don't you think?" Raphael asked. "Why would anyone want to do that?"

Tafari poured another drink for each of them. "I don't know why, but I know it happens. I worked doing it. It was my job when I was a kid in La Nouvelle, France. We created a thin film on silicon wafers using really high temperatures. I think they said it was, like, 1,200 degrees centigrade. Those were the discs used for the quartz generators."

Gold asked, "You mean like for the air controller and my blender and stuff like that?"

"Right, but we also put it in food. It's just sand, you know. I was told it could store a charge, block a current, and even limit the flow of electrical current, but the most important part was it could create an electrical charge inside the human body. I think it had to be kept at a constant temperature to work, like 98.6." She smiled, but her face was serious.

Now Raphael was interested. "Were you told why we would need an electrical charge in our bodies? I mean, we already have electrical charges in the synapses of our nerve endings and in our brains."

"No. I never found out. Like I said, I was just a kid. I started wheezing one day, and my father made them give me a different job." She poured another drink, and Raphael sipped his first one, marveling at how much liquor such a young girl could put away, and that she had a father who could make the Republic give his daughter a new job.

She gulped and added, "I did hear later, when I was working at the Bureau of Information, that the charge has to do with what happens when your TV is on but not broadcasting, and it has to do with the meditations."

"What about the meditations?" Raphael asked.

"We need to communicate, and it takes more of a charge than the human body can muster." She took another swig of her drink and pulled off her halter top nonchalantly. "It's hot," she explained.

"What did you mean by calling me a Neanderthal?" Gold teased.

"Well, I guess because you sort of are, at least part. You all are. Almost all human beings have a small percentage of Neanderthal genetics."

"How do you know all this?" Raphael asked, genuinely impressed.

"I come from a whole family of geneticists," she answered and smiled.

"And you?" Morgan asked. "Can you lay claim to being a geneticist too?"

"No, but I've picked up a bit over the years. Can you imagine sitting around the table with a bunch of people who know your entire DNA? Made for fun dinners."

"Right," said Gold, as he returned to his drink.

"You know, it's funny," Raphael said, fighting desperately not to stare at her body. "How did we get where we are now?"

"You mean how did you get from cave men to civilization?" Tafari asked.

"I guess."

"To hear my family tell it, it's all genetics. Stuff is changed, evolves. People change with it."

"But to come so far in, what… forty thousand years?" Raphael asked, sipping his drink.

"You have no idea," Tafari said. "You should hear my family talk about it. And it's a lot longer than forty thousand years. A lot longer."

Gold jumped back into the conversation. "I suppose you're going to tell us we haven't come far from the Neanderthal, right?"

"Well, no. There is a big difference, huge difference, but not how you might think."

"So how?" asked Raphael, his interest growing. "Evolution? God?"

"Sex," Tafari superimposed the word over the two Raphael had suggested.

"Can we have another drink?" Morgan asked, "and let's get off this subject. It's boring. I think we should investigate this storm. I don't want to be walking home in eighty-mile-an-hour winds and hail. I got caught in that a couple of weeks ago and it hurt."

Tafari leaned across Gold and snatched up the remote to the TV, turned it up, then jumped up and went into the bathroom.

"Being the fourth storm this month, everyone should be all set," said the African announcer.

"Aren't we at war with Africa?" Gold asked. "What's she doing on the tube?"

"It's not really a tube anymore," Raphael said, putting his drink down on the floor in front of him.

"Do you think she's a conspiracy theorist? You know, the TV is watching us stuff," Gold asked the other two, nodding toward the bathroom. "Hey, did you notice she turns it off? I thought we weren't supposed to do that." There was no answer since she was stepping back into the room.

"She's new," Raphael said. Nodding at the announcer on TV. "I believe she is from one of the liberated countries. Chad, I think."

"She'd be perfect to run for president," Morgan said, smiling to her friends. They laughed. "Did you know Carleen keeps trying to put Entitleds into government posts? I've caught it twice. Why the hell would she want to do that?"

"We've had four now, right?" asked Gold.

"Right," said Raphael. "Four blacks, but never a black woman."

Tafari returned. "I like being down here," she said. "I have buildings on both sides of me. One is three stories and the other five, and the wind doesn't usually hit me at all. The rain is the real problem."

"I have a question," Gold interrupted. The three turned to him.

"Where do you work now?"

"I don't work." Tafari smiled. "I think the Republic feels my family produces plenty, and there is no need for their little girl to be employed."

"I think we should get going," Morgan suggested, pulling herself up and watching both Gold and Raphael glancing at the pink underwear she couldn't hide while wearing her short dress. "Maybe it is for him tonight," she thought. Her glance hovered on her old friend for an extra second, letting him know that she had seen him looking. Embarrassed, Raphael hustled to help her up and purposefully looked away as he did. They said their goodbyes, and Morgan kissed Tafari good night, smiled to Barry Gold, who was obviously staying behind, and the two friends stepped back into the alleyway. Many of the shop lights were still on, and the powdery mist and swirling wind created concentric waves of multi colors in the air. The friends walked side by side in silence for a while, and then Raphael spoke, still looking at the ground in front of his feet. "Do you think there is something in what she says about the televisions?"

"I don't know. I doubt it. I think it might have been the absinthe talking."

They walked nearly another mile in silence, entering onto Republic Avenue. "Mine broke down a few months ago, and when I reported it, there was another one at my door within an hour, and the guys who brought it hooked it up right away."

"So?"

"So, I don't know, it seemed pretty efficient for the electric company." Raphael chuckled. "Back about ten years ago when my old TV broke down, they didn't even bother to take it with them. They just brought a new one, hooked it up and left the old one. I had to bring it down eighteen flights to the basement and store it."

The wind began to pick up and once even blew Morgan a few running steps ahead of him. She grabbed the wrought iron rail in front of her doorway. She lived about a mile from Raphael's place in a first story, six-room apartment, but the wind's intensity was growing, and small hailstones started bouncing off the roofs, tents, and tarps between the multi-storied buildings.

"You should stay," Morgan said, turning toward Raphael. "The storm is here."

A small metal sign that had been ripped from its pole skimmed down the center of the street as if in agreement with Morgan, even though he noticed her looking back down the street and not at the sign at all.

"Maybe so," he said, and she held the door open for him, still looking into the blackness behind them. As they became comfortable inside the doorway, she asked, "Did you notice him?"

"I did," Raphael said, pulling back the curtain on the door

and looking back outside into the darkness. "Was it the guy from the sandwich truck?"

"I don't think so. I think it might have been the first guy with the suspenders."

"What did he say to you?"

She shook off the rain from her coat. "I didn't really hear him, but I think he was inviting us inside that bar near the alley. Maybe he lives around here." She spun toward the kitchen. "Nightcap?" she asked over her shoulder, but Raphael didn't need one. Instead, they went to bed and enjoyed each other for the night.

# Chapter Five

*"Grant what eyes of angels have not [seen] what ears of rulers have not heard, and what has not arisen in the human heart, which became angelic, made in the image of the animate God when it was formed in the beginning."*

*- Prayer of the Apostle Paul, Nag Hammadi scriptures, Codex II*

Gold was excited as he hustled into the seventh-floor office of Morgan Baez early Monday morning. He closed the door behind himself, and, surprising Baez, he quickly sat on a chair in front of her desk. It had been raining hard this morning, and his walk to work had soaked his clothes and hair, and as he sat before her, Baez craned her neck sideways to look at the growing puddle on her floor.

"I had an interesting time after the two of you left the other night," he began.

"Okay?" Morgan questioned.

There was a pause that went on just a little too long and Morgan prodded, "So are you going to tell me or am I just supposed to guess?"

"No, I'm going to tell you. I just don't know where to start."

"Well, I'm kind of busy to hear about your sexual exploits right now, maybe over lunch? You know you're wet, right?"

"Of course I do. It's not about sex… but that was unbelievable. She knew stuff, wow… some other time though. This is about something else." He gathered his thoughts and began, "Well, we drank most of that bottle of absinthe and…"

"Not now," Morgan dismissed him. "I think some other time, huh?"

"No, Morgan, this is important." His frightened eyes didn't look now like a man about to discuss his new girlfriend, so Baez sat back and allowed him to go on.

"She told me, as if she had been there, that after the worldwide conflict in the mid-twenty-first century the government was taken over by one family. One really rich family. They just bought it up and tossed everyone else out. She said from there on they ruled everything."

"So, your new girlfriend told you this? Your, what, twenty-three-year-old girlfriend who has no job, lives in the Entitleds zone, and drinks absinthe like it was water told you this, and you believed it? Did you know that stuff used to be illegal to drink?"

"That's what I'm trying to tell you. That's why she has no job. It was her family. This one family is 'The Republic.'"

Morgan was just about to toss him when he asked, "When did you learn the rules?"

"I don't know," Morgan answered as if it mattered not at all.

"That's right," Gold said. "None of us knows."

"Wait a minute," Baez said. She picked up her phone, and after a silent second, she said, "Raphael, could you come up here? Yes. Right now."

As she hung up, Gold started to talk again but was shushed by a wave of her finger.

A few minutes later, Raphael entered the office.

"Close the door, and try to avoid the puddle," Morgan suggested. What Gold saw as of paramount importance, Morgan apparently saw as a chance to tease her friend and thought Raphael might also enjoy it.

"Raphael, when did you learn the rules?" she asked.

"When I was a kid, I guess."

Gold broke in. "No, really. Think about it. When did you learn the rules? Was it from your mother or from a school? When exactly?"

"I don't really remember. Why?"

"I have one more question for both of you. When did you start liking the Patriots?"

"What?"

"Humor me, Morgan."

"When did you start liking the Patriots, Raphael?"

"A long time ago."

"Morgan, how about you?"

"Years ago. Same time you both did."

"I thought that too, but then I found something in my pocket today because I wore a suit I hadn't worn since last week."

"Okay," Morgan said, dismissing the questions. "I have to get back to work."

Gold was serious. There was no humor in his speech. "Morgan, listen to me. I thought I loved the Patriots too, for years, but I found this in my pocket this morning."

He handed a piece of paper to Raphael. "Look at the date," Gold hinted, pointing at the betting slip.

Raphael read it and looked up in surprise. "Why the hell would you do this? The Pats are sure money." He handed the slip to Morgan.

As she furrowed her brow and looked up at Gold, he said, "Right, I bet a hundred on the Mercantiles… last week."

He looked back and forth at his friends to see that they understood that it was common knowledge that Barry Gold made half his money on gambling. He only made sure bets. "Why the hell would I do that? We only started loving this team this week. And if you remember, no one could figure out at our last meeting when we had started not hating them."

Morgan and Raphael looked at each other, finally interested in what Gold had to say.

"Now, are you ready to listen to what my drunken girlfriend told me after you left?"

"Okay," Morgan said, "Go ahead."

"She said we learned the rules from the TV. We each, every person, learn the rules when we first begin watching the television, same thing with the football stuff. She said the Republic used to be a political party. There were two, a Democrat Party and a Republican party. She called them the elephants and the donkeys, but after the Worldwide Conflict, the Republicans were taken over by a family, her family, and they changed everything. And to make people go along with them, they introduced the silicon dioxide into the food, the connection to the TV, and the rules."

"Wait, wait, wait, hold on," Raphael interjected. "What is this nonsense about sand in our food?"

"She said silicon dioxide creates electricity, and it was needed for some reason, so we would do what we are told by the damn television. Even you agreed it was in a lot of stuff. She told me the electrical charge was to bolster receptors that were genetically placed inside our bodies and that they picked up the signals from the TV during the meditations. We were taught the rules without ever being taught the rules. They were just, what did she say, 'implanted divinely' into our brains or something."

Morgan stood up and began to shoo the boys out of her office, but Raphael had a few questions first and did not move. "And the Patriots? Even if we believed we were being electronically manipulated by some family somewhere, why would this almighty family care what football team we cheered for?"

"I asked her that too. She said it was just a test. Everyone hated the damn team up until last week, and the family, the damn Republic, was testing the whole system again. She said there were some changes made and they wanted to see if it still worked, so they chose the team everyone hated. Made us all love them overnight." Gold looked from one to the other, then added, "I made some calls. People in Dallas and Pittsburg now love the Patriots. For God's sake, man, I called my brother in New York, and he loves the Patriots."

"That's crazy," Morgan said and looked to her friend, "Raphael, tell him. That's insane."

Raphael looked at his friend. It didn't look as if he was joking.

"Are you serious? Someone in New York loves the Patriots? That is insane."

"Okay," said Gold, "laugh if you want, but it's not funny. Tafari is older than you think." He looked from one friend to another. "She says she is a lot older."

"Okay, how much older?"

"I don't know, Morgan, but she remembers stuff that happened a long time ago."

"Barry, I think you need to listen to Morgan. This is sounding a bit like that absinthe did a number on your heads."

"Okay, back to work," Baez, now the supervisor again, her fun over, stood and shooed them out.

"We'll go visit her tonight. She can tell you herself. She makes it really believable," Gold said.

"Sure, sure," Morgan said by way of dismissal. "We'll all

go." After a short pause, Morgan said, "I kind of like her." She laughed, which made Gold cringe and Raphael smile.

Safely back at his desk, Raphael began working on his new characterization of the presidential candidate.

He thought, "*I guess I have to know what goal he would have, first, before anything else. A call to greatness always works for votes.*"

"Make the USR great," he typed. "Create more friends than enemies around the world…. continue the freebies and add to them, maybe free internet like in the old days. Food, better USR food packages… Safety." *The truth*, he thought, *is that we already feel pretty safe. It is only Africa and Mexico and South America who feel a little threatened.* "Maybe we could end one of those wars… one at a time."

"Is that the characterization?" Morgan asked peering over his shoulder.

"Damn, you startled me." Raphael smiled. "Yes, I was just thinking, well, something came to me. I guess we have to show he has a way to answer the questions who are we, where are we going and how the hell we're going to get there…. Then twist it all to make sure the Entitleds will vote for it."

"Hain't we got all the fools in town on our side?" she said, referring to the writer Mark Twain from her college ancient literature class.

"And hain't that a big enough majority in any town?" Raphael answered, and they both laughed.

"So, you took ancient lit too?"

"No," Raphael said, furrowing his brow. "I don't know where I learned that. Maybe the microwave."

"Don't get crazy. You probably heard me say it a thousand times. It's my favorite quote."

"Yeah, you're right. So, when are we going tonight?"

"Meet you down at Le Renard again? Six? Tell Gold."

Before leaving work for the day, Raphael phoned his friend, and Gold agreed to meeting at six in the afternoon. Raphael hurried home to clean up and change. He wasn't sure why he was doing it. He wondered if he was doing it for Morgan. She had looked good during their last meeting, and he kept getting glimpses of her struggling to stand up and damn near exposing herself. Whatever it was, he knew he was thinking of her more often now, and when he did, she was always leading him to a good place, a comfortable place.

He was disappointed when he approached the restaurant, and both of his friends were already there. They had both come directly from work and Morgan was dressed in an unrevealing suit with a long skirt, and her hair was up. Gold was anxious. "Let's hurry up," he said the second Raphael arrived, and they turned and walked three-across toward the Entitleds zone and Tafari's apartment. Gold was moving so fast that they were all sweating in the unseasonably hot afternoon.

"Damn. I wish I could make some genetic modification to thin my blood out so I could take this heat better," Raphael said, wiping his brow.

"It's only a little… a few blocks." Gold sped up.

Morgan and Raphael exchanged looks of dismay at each other and hurried to catch him. As they turned the corner near the sandwich truck, the young man smiled, but quickly ducked inside the bar behind him.

"It's probably air conditioned in there," Raphael said to no one, but Gold was already knocking on Tafari's door. There was no answer. He knocked again, a little more insistently. Then again. There was no answer. From behind them came a voice with a distinct French accent, "Tafari is visiting."

The three turned and were surprised to see the long-haired man with the white derby hat. Today he was wearing the red mask and bright blue bell-bottom pants held up with red suspenders. He still had no shirt. They stood stunned. "She is visiting her father," he said again. "You should go."

Raphael nodded silently. Morgan lost no time in pushing past him and hurried up the alley and out to the street. Gold followed, looking back at the strange man. When they were all once again on the sidewalk, Morgan turned to the two men. "Look, I'm hungry. Let's get something to eat somewhere. Gold, you're buying."

They worked over dinner at a small food barn that served hamburgers, tacos, and spaghetti and meatballs. Morgan took a large ravenous bite and as soon as it was swallowed, she said, "I don't like this new Merle guy."

"You mean the new appointee for the Water Department?"

"Right."

"But he's already been married off to an Asian woman he

doesn't even like."

Morgan snapped her attention toward Gold. "Why do you think he doesn't like her?" she asked.

"Well, for one thing, because he's gay," said Gold without looking up from his meal.

"Get a new guy… and you know what, make it a woman."

"Okay," Raphael answered, taking a long drink of iced tea, "Do you mind if she's Asian and married to Merle?"

Gold laughed. Morgan nodded.

They finished their meals while Morgan continued to attack Raphael's choices. "And that presidential characterization, I don't like that either."

"What about it don't you like? Save it! I'll be right back," Raphael answered, and standing up, craned his neck in search of the men's room. Morgan and Gold were laughing when he returned to the table.

"What's so funny?" he asked.

"Nothing," said Gold. "We were just talking about Trudy's blouse the other day. I thought Will was going to have a stroke."

"Yeah, it was a bit much," Raphael answered. He thought about taking another bite of the half-eaten burger but instead pushed it away, wiped his mouth, and asked, "So Morgan, what don't you like about our president?"

"Start over," she said sharply. "The one you showed me isn't good enough. We want to win this one by a landslide. We want everyone to want this candidate. It's important."

"Why so?" asked Raphael.

"Just is," she said and abruptly stood from the table. "I have to get going."

"Me too," Gold added, and Raphael nearly stood up but stopped himself. "You know, I think I might have a drink. It's hot out there. See you both tomorrow."

Truth was, Raphael didn't like his friend when she got like this. He felt that when they left work, she should stop being the boss and just be his friend, but there were times when she would be silent for a few seconds, her mood would change abruptly, and she would launch into something like she just had as if she had gotten a telephone call from a superior.

Raphael watched his friends leave. Outside, as they passed the front window, Morgan looked quickly back in his direction. She smiled apologetically but continued down the street.

Raphael motioned to the waitress. When she arrived, he politely asked her to clear the table and bring him a vodka tonic. He turned his chair so he could see the television over the bar in the corner and began to watch a silent version of the news. For a few dollars, you could slide your card at the table and use the ear plugs to listen to what was on TV or use the laptop television built into the middle of the table, but he really didn't want to listen. The picture was something to occupy his mind without really paying attention. He felt a presence standing beside him and turned to get his drink from the waitress, but instead it was Trudy.

"Trudy," he said in happy surprise. "Here, sit down," he

said, pushing out the chair that had been Gold's with his foot. She sat and smiled. Now this was more like it. He knew how young she was. He knew his own age, and he knew nothing would come of this, but he also knew she was a tremendous pleasure to just look at.

"What are you doing here?" he asked.

"I was walking by and saw you sitting all alone, so I thought I'd come in and say hi. Hi."

The waitress arrived with Raphael's drink, and Trudy smiled up at her. "Could I have an absinthe and cranberry juice?"

Raphael was shocked at her order because of her age but made no judgment.

"So, Trudy, what have you been up to?"

"Not much. You pretty much see everything that is me." Trudy smiled a perfectly white smile, and for a second Raphael was lost in her brown eyes. Her leg brushed against his, and she quickly apologized.

"Right," he finally answered as her drink arrived. "So, not much after work, huh?"

"No, I just enjoy walking around until it gets dark. I like the streets, the people. I shop a lot. You?"

"I don't do much shopping. Is that something you bought?" he asked, pointing at the pendant hanging from her neck and resting in the cleavage between her breasts.

"This? No, my friend gave this to me. It's a gift." She leaned over the table so Raphael could get a good look, and he realized she was flirting.

"Beautiful," Raphael said, gazing up at her wide eyes.

"Do you know what it's made out of?" Trudy leaned over further, clearly trying to show him a close up.

"I think it's quartz," he answered before sipping his drink.

Trudy sat back and downed her entire drink in one swallow, took a breath, and placed the glass on the table as if it were going to break.

"Whoa," Raphael cautioned, "Take it easy. That stuff is really potent."

"Me too," she said with a smile.

There was a second chain hanging lower on her neck, and whatever was hanging from it was hiding between her breasts and below the top of her blouse.

"What do you have hidden there?" Raphael asked, pointing with his thumb at whatever was hiding at the end of the chain. She may be a kid, but he was not content to allow her the only double entendre at the table.

"Mr. Aronson, I think you're flirting with me." After a pause, understanding flashed on her face. "Oh, you mean my ring." Tugging on the chain, the girl pulled a ring that hung from the chain out from its hiding place.

"Is that gold?" Raphael asked, now curious about the surprisingly old looking ring.

"Oh no. It might be plated, but I doubt it's gold. It was a gift too. Do you know what it is?" she asked, getting up and coming around the table to stand next to Raphael. She leaned over again so he could take the ring in his hand. He turned it from side to side and held it closer to his face. The ring had a roundish gold face with the bust of a warrior on it. Around his head were the words *Childirici Regis*.

"I don't know," he said, now more interested in the ring than in the show-off teenager's advances. "We could look it up on the tabletop." He slid his card, and the laptop attached to the table lit up.

"Do you know anything about quartz?" she asked him as he logged on.

"Very little. I think it's a mineral, and it is part of your pendant."

"Have you ever heard this name, Childirici?"

"No. Where'd you get it?"

"An admirer." She smiled and sat back down.

"Well," Raphael said after a few minutes of research. "It seems this is a replica of a ring that was owned by a Merovingian king. Seems he was a pretty badass king, too. He defeated the Visigoths back in 463 AD. Then he beat the Goths. It says he was buried with this ring, so I guess this is definitely a replica. It's nice, though. Did a boy give this to you?"

"Yes."

"Was he French?"

"Why?"

"Because according to what I'm reading, he was a French king, the son of Merovech, who started the Merovingian Dynasty. So, I figure it would be a French boy who gave it to you."

"It was." Trudy sat up a little in her chair and looked across at Raphael with her head tilted to one side. "Mr. Aronson?"

"Yes, Trudy."

"Would you like to sleep with me tonight?"

He was not shocked. He was surprised, but despite that, he managed a smile. "I would love to, but you are a little young for me, and I don't think it would be right."

"Okay. I was just asking. Are you sure?" She was now standing beside the table, her leg brushing against his arm.

"I'm afraid I'm sure, Trudy. You deserve someone your own age."

"There are so few men my age," she smiled. "And I like men. Are you positive?"

"See you tomorrow, Trudy."

She smiled and walked out of the restaurant. She waved playfully from the window as she left.

"Weird kid," Raphael said to himself. Even with the changing times and sex seemingly becoming almost a priority for existence, Trudy's advance was out of place, he thought. He allowed himself a brief fantasy, but then Raphael finished his drink and walked home through the relative coolness of the evening. He could feel the comfort of the slumbering city, the communal safety of the darkened streets. A dog lashed out at him from behind a wrought-iron fence that his owners had put him behind for the protection of other people. At the Radisson Building, he stopped after climbing to the fifth or sixth floor and looked out at the darkened city, lit only by the moon. It was a beautiful place at night, when no one was plotting, sneaking, hiding, when the only thing on the minds of most was to slip into a subconscious state and sleep, dream, and refresh before getting back to their jobs.

# CHAPTER SIX

While still fumbling to unlock his apartment door, Raphael heard the shrill sound of the phone ringing. He made it inside before it stopped and picked the receiver off the wall cradle in the kitchen.

"Hello?" Raphael thought it was late for a phone call.

"Raphael?" Gold was out of breath.

"What's the matter, Barry?"

"I was followed. I think I was followed. There's a guy outside. I think it's the crazy guy from the bar."

"Whoa, slow down. First, should I come over?"

"No. I don't think so. But something's wrong. I went back to see Tafari."

Raphael sat down on a kitchen chair and switched the phone to his better ear. "And?"

"And she told me some other things, and then warned

me… when I told her we had to work together and tell people, she warned me not to."

"What do you mean, she warned you? Wait a minute, what did she tell you?"

"She told me to look up the parable of the mustard seed. From the Bible. She said I should read 'The Gospel of Thomas.'"

"There is no Gospel of Thomas," Raphael replied.

"Of course there is. Tafari told me, The Gospel of Thomas."

"Okay," Raphael said. He was beginning to think his friend had gotten into the bottle of absinthe again.

"She said we were going to be 'harvested.' She said the parable isn't about plants. The smallest seed isn't really a mustard seed. That was just what people would understand at the time."

"I think you might want to sleep it off. What do you think?"

"I think I believe her."

"Me too, buddy. She's pretty hot, huh? Why don't you get some sleep?"

"A guy followed me home. He was outside, across the street."

"Is he there now?"

"Let me look." After a short silence, Gold was back on the phone. "No, I think he's gone. I think it was that crazy guy with the stupid hat from the other night."

"Okay, get some sleep. See you in the morning."

Raphael hung up the phone, glanced out his window at the silent street, and then went to bed.

Barry Gold went back to look out the window into the shadows. "Don't be paranoid," he said to himself.

# Chapter Seven

*"All the emanations from the father are fullness, and all his emanations find their root in the one who caused them all to grow from himself."*

*- The Gospel of Truth - Nag Hammadi scriptures Codex I*

The air in the conference room was stifling, almost unbreathable, so Raphael opened a window and looked out over the city. He thought it looked more dangerous today, out from under the cover of darkness. The morning mist filtered the sunshine into a veil, and behind it, the city was waking up. Lone or nearly alone stragglers walked slowly toward their jobs. Dogs hurried their way into the shadows, their nightly free reign dwindling, and the heat was beginning to reflect off the tin rooftops of the makeshift hovels between the old buildings. The city was deteriorating, and not slowly.

"Kind of a mess, isn't it?" Carleen, his coworker, offered, standing just off his shoulder and looking out over New Clovis.

"It seemed much more friendly last night," Raphael answered.

"I guess when you can't see everything, you can pretend it's not there," Carleen said. They laughed a little, turned from the window, and sat down at the conference table as the others filtered in ready for an update on Raphael's presidential characterization.

Morgan was late, and the others became fidgety since she had never been late before. Morgan always seemed to know innately what she was to do and when she was to do it, as if her calendar was in her head rather than in her computer. She was never late.

She didn't even apologize as she entered the room, turned her back to the others to close the door, turned away from them as she walked to her chair, and when she turned around, they could see why. As unfathomable as it was, Morgan Baez had been crying. Raphael stood from his chair, looked at his friend, then turned to the rest of the conference participants and said, "We'll do this later." Then he motioned softly for them to leave the room. When the room was empty except for the two of them, she turned her face up to him.

"Barry is dead," she said incredulously.

His first thought was that, of course Gold wasn't dead; he had just talked to him on the phone a few hours ago.

"What?"

"He fell out of his window. Twelve stories up. He's dead."

She looked into Raphael's eyes. She tried to speak again, but even though her mouth moved, no words came out.

"Maybe you should take the day off," Raphael said. She looked at him, and he nodded his encouragement.

"Maybe," she said. "I'll get my stuff and go."

Raphael was torn between the death of one friend and the sadness of another. He decided he would deal first with the one who was still alive, despite the questions racing through his mind. "How did you find out?" he asked.

"Trudy heard it somewhere. She told me." Morgan rose and left the room.

Raphael thought the teenage girl might be having a hard time with this too. She was at her desk when he approached to see if she was alright.

"Hi, Mr. Aronson," she said without any hint of emotion. She actually smiled at him.

"Trudy, where did you hear about Barry?"

"It's kind of strange. A friend of his called this morning. I was the only one here, so I answered the phone, and she told me about it. She said he fell from his balcony last night. She said he had been drinking a lot."

Raphael thought for a few seconds. He too had thought his friend had probably been drinking when he had called last night, but not enough to fall out of his window.

"Trudy, I need you to help me with something. Do you have some time today?"

She nodded. "What can I do?"

"Do you know his password?"

She did. Raphael never asked how she knew it but supposed it would be possible since Trudy worked right across from Gold. They were friendly, and she could see his computer from her chair, so it was very possible she had picked up his password in the course of time. They went across to his desk, and she opened the laptop. His screen saver was a picture of a petrified forest. It was labeled at the bottom: *Petrified Forest on the Isle of Lesbos.*

"That's new," Raphael said, as Tafari's words came back to him from their conversation at her house. *"It's a beautiful island, you know, Lesbos. It is covered with flowers and olive trees and there is an amazing tropical forest in the northwest part of the island. It is one of the most enchanting parts of Greece."*

"Okay, Trudy, I need you to get me everything you can about silicon dioxide."

"Silicon dioxide? Everything? Why? What is it?"

"It has to do with the characterization I'm working on. Can you do it?"

"Sure. I'll have it for you." She hesitated, waiting for more instructions from him.

"This afternoon, okay?"

"Okay." She smiled to herself as she walked back to her desk, and Raphael sat down at Gold's computer. He had to see what he could find.

He began opening folders on the desktop. There was a picture Barry had taken of himself and Tafari on her couch, what Tafari called "a selfie." Gold looked happy, and Raphael shook his head, thinking what a waste it had been for his friend to die so young. "Harvested," Raphael recalled his friend saying. The picture was interesting in its anachronistic sort of way. Raphael hadn't noticed the throw-back accoutrements of the apartment while he was there, but now saw them in the picture. The green velvety couch itself was old, maybe older than a hundred years. It had an ice chest built into it. Raphael could tell that because the chest was open, and he could see several bottles. The chair next to it was of ornate wrought iron. It seemed old and French, but it also seemed to fold in the middle. Some of the pillows they had all sat on were on the couch, and directly behind the couch Raphael could see wall-hanging rugs on the back wall. Where one ended and another began, he could see a picture sticking out from behind the rug on the right, and he wondered why anyone would have pictures behind a wall rug. He laughed a bit at Tafari's eccentricities. So strange for such a young woman, he thought. He clicked off the picture and clicked onto another folder marked *Photo*.

The picture was dark, but because of the moonlight Raphael could figure out what it was. He enlarged it and could tell it was a street, and the picture was taken from high above. In the center was a figure, just light enough so Raphael could make out the hair.

"Shit," he said and clicked off the picture.

Raphael turned to Trudy. Seeing her hard at work, he turned back to Gold's computer. Gold had been telling the truth. He was sure of it. There was something going on here that involved silicon dioxide, televisions, the rules, the Patriots, where and even when Tafari was from. And his friend had been warned not to get involved, and now he was dead. Raphael wondered if the telephone call from Gold had gotten him "harvested," whatever the hell that meant.

His head was swimming; mustard seed, Gospel of Thomas, the picture at Tafari's, silicon dioxide, the television, the rules, the Patriots, and Tafari's family. Who exactly is the Republic? What is the goal of all this? He double-clicked on a folder marked *Thomas*. "He must have done this from home last night," Raphael said under his breath.

"What?" Trudy asked.

"Nothing. I was just thinking Barry must have done a lot of work last night after he called me."

"He called you?" she asked.

"He was worried that someone had followed him home."

"Did someone?"

Raphael knew the answer, but for some reason he decided to keep it to himself. "I don't know."

The file he had just opened was more interesting than the last one, and Raphael gave it his full attention. The file contained notes from Gold, and the date supported Raphael's guess that it had been done last night from home. It read: *Gospel of Thomas, 80 AD: found at Nag Hamadi – twin brother to Jesus – doubting Thomas – left out of Bible – earlier than new test - not meant to be literal… 3-9-10-20-21-29-40-57-65-70-*

*73-84-113-114.*

"What the hell are these numbers? Trudy, look at this, will you?"

The girl happily came across and, placing a hand softly on Raphael's shoulder, peered at the screen of Gold's computer.

"Got any idea what the numbers are?" he asked.

"I haven't any idea," she finally said. Then, after a second, she added, "Maybe they are verse numbers in this Gospel of Thomas." She stood up and returned to her own work.

Another folder was labeled *mustard seed.* He clicked on it, wondering what the hell was going on.

*The disciples said to Jesus, "Tell us what the Kingdom of Heaven is like." He said to them, "It is like a mustard seed, the smallest of all seeds. But when it falls on tilled soil, it produces a great plant and becomes a shelter for birds of the sky."*

Under the quote Gold had typed, "What is the smallest seed of all?"

"Jesus Christ, Barry, what are you getting religious now?" Raphael's confusion had multiplied as he tried another folder named *Smallest of all Seeds.*

*Jesus said, "Now the sower went out, took a handful (of seeds), and scattered them. Some fell on the road; the birds came and gathered them up. Others fell on the rock, did not take root*

*in the soil and did not produce ears. And others fell on thorns; they choked the seed(s) and worms ate them. And others fell on the good soil and produced good fruit: it bore sixty per measure and a hundred and twenty per measure."*

Gold had left a note here too: "the age of humans. We're the good soil. Genetics." It was all he said. Raphael closed the file and sat back. He inserted a flash drive and copied all the folders on Gold's computer. He sat back and watched it download, his mind racing.

"How's your sandcastle coming?" he asked Trudy. "Find anything?"

"Pretty close to done," she answered. Raphael took a quick look at his watch. He hadn't realized how much time had gone by, but it was nearly the end of the day. He rose from his desk and headed for the coffee room. "You want anything from the break room?" he asked the girl.

"A black would be nice," she answered without looking up. "Coffee," she added with a quick, flirty smile.

"Damn," thought Raphael. "The girl's got a one-track mind."

He went unrushed to the break room, pushed the right buttons, and took the coffee with cream and sugar from the machine, wondering why Stofe always brought his own cream and sugar when he could get it right here. Then he pushed the buttons for Trudy's black coffee. With both coffees poured, he sat down at a table. No one else was in the break room, and the death of his friend was beginning to settle in. He couldn't take his mind off the photo of the street below Gold's apartment. It was the redhead.

Why would Tafari lie about being there? Did she kill his friend? Could it have truly been an accident? Whichever way this had happened, he intended to find out why the girl had lied, and he wanted to make sure Gold had not been murdered for something he had stumbled on, something that the same girl had told him. He took stock of who he could trust. Of course, there was Morgan, and he assumed he could trust Trudy. He thought for a few minutes. Possibly Carleen. That's it. No one else.

As Raphael rose to return to Gold's computer, Trudy entered the break room with a printout of her day's work on silicon dioxide. "This is pretty interesting stuff," she said as she sat at the table, slid the report across to him, and picked up her coffee. She sipped it while looking at him. "What did you find?" she asked.

"I don't know," Raphael said as if he was just now coming to that conclusion himself. "It seems my friend was becoming religious." He looked across the table, assessing the girl. Just as his stare was becoming a little too long, he made a decision and leaned back in his chair. "I did find something though. A picture of someone outside Barry's apartment last night—someone who shouldn't have been there."

"Who?"

"A girl named Tafari. Someone I believe he just met a few nights ago."

"So why shouldn't she have been there?" Trudy asked, putting down her coffee. "Wait a minute. Tafari, that is the name of the woman who called this morning to tell me Mr. Gold had jumped out his window. And strangely, she called him Associate Gold. Was Mr. Gold an Associate? I didn't know that."

"No, he was a Member. She said he jumped?"

"I don't know. Maybe she said he fell, but she didn't say how she knew."

"He called me last night," Raphael said. "And he said a man had followed him home, but the picture he took last night and forwarded to his work computer was of the girl standing across the street. If it wasn't for the moonlight, I wouldn't have been able to recognize her."

Raphael picked up the report Trudy had finished and began to leaf through it. "What did you find in all this?"

"Well, I could have been more specific if you told me what you were looking for."

Raphael put the report down. "Can silicon dioxide hold an electrical charge?" he asked.

"Yes."

"Can it emit an electrical charge?"

"Yes."

"Can it power a transmitter of some kind?"

"I think it can." Trudy said sliding her chair around the table so she was sitting next to Raphael and turning pages in an effort to find a certain page, "Here it is," she said after a minute and began to read, "'Silicon dioxide is piezoelectric and when it is stressed, it builds up an electrical charge.' It says in here somewhere that it can be used as a microphone or a phonograph." She looked up from the paper to Raphael. "So I assume it can power a transmitter of some kind too."

Raphael pondered the new information, thinking about what his friend had told him on the phone. "What about if it was, like, inside the human body? Could it actually transmit a signal?" he asked her.

"Hold on, wait a minute. I did see something like that." Trudy fingered through the pages and Raphael became nervously aware that her leg was pressed firmly against his. He moved a little so they weren't touching, and she arrived at the spot in the report she had been seeking.

"Here it is." She pointed to a paragraph halfway down the page and slid the report in front of him.

He read the passage out loud. "The electronic circuit is an oscillator and an amplifier whose output passes through the quartz resonator. The resonator acts as an electric filter, eliminating all but the single frequency of interest. The output of the resonator feeds back to the input of the amplifier, and the resonator assures that the oscillator 'howls' with the exact frequency of interest. When the circuit starts up, even a single shot can cascade to bringing the oscillator at the desired frequency."

Trudy interrupted and pressed her leg against him again, "And there is something in here about constant temperatures keeping the frequency stable. Here it is: 'The most obvious way of reducing the effect of temperature on oscillation rate is to keep the crystal at a constant temperature.'" She looked up at Raphael, who was lost in his thoughts. He repeated what

Tafari had said the first night he had met her. "Like 98.6," he remembered out loud. "Thanks, Trudy. Look, I appreciate what you've done here, but I'm not sure you should help anymore."

"Why not?" she asked and pouted.

"I'm not sure it's safe," Raphael explained.

"I'm in. I kind of liked Mr. Gold. This is about his death, right?"

Raphael nodded.

"Then I want to help."

"Okay, but nothing more until I speak with Morgan. Tomorrow. I'll let you know if we are going to continue with this."

"Tomorrow," she answered, her tone more of a demand than an assent.

"Tomorrow," Raphael repeated.

# Chapter Eight



*- The Holy Bible, John, 8:37*

Trudy left Raphael Aronson alone in the building in the blazing heat of the afternoon and walked briskly down Enterprise purposefully toward the "adult section" of the Entitleds zone. She passed a few open-door bars that were teeming with people and noise. At one door, a patron, a large bald man with an earring, reached out and grabbed her arm. "Where do you think you're going, little girl?"

Trudy stopped. She didn't struggle but only looked directly into the man's eyes. "You don't want to do this," she said evenly, and she smiled.

The bald man looked back for a second or two and let go of

her arm. "Sorry," he said. "I thought you were someone else."

"Of course you did." She smiled again and walked on.

Then at the door of a bar called "Rule 20" she entered. "Go Patriots," she said to no one as she crossed the threshold. She walked to the bar where a young woman was sitting. Trudy looked at the drink sitting in front of the other woman. "I'll have one of those," she said and sat down at the bar. "Do I know you?" she asked the woman. Once an emotion took hold in her, she had to extinguish it. This had been the downfall of her kind.

※ ※

Raphael returned to Gold's desk, looking through everything he could find on the computer. Most of it was work related, but here and there were files and folders that didn't have anything to do with work. He clicked on one marked *Method*.

The first line read,

*"music, social media, computer, phones, clocks"*

The next line said only,

*"television."*

The third line said,

*"television, rules transmitted, silicon dioxide, rules received?????*

*Who is sending????*

"That's a good question," Raphael said out loud. "And what is being sent?"

The footsteps made it about halfway down the central hallway before Raphael remembered he was supposedly alone in the building except for the guard downstairs. He got up from the desk and began to step into the hallway when he decided it might be better to wait and see who it was. He listened, determined from which direction the steps were coming, and then he positioned himself next to the door on the side where he wouldn't be seen by someone walking from right to left down the hall but where he could plainly see who it was as they passed by. The sound wasn't the click-click of high heels, and based on the heaviness of the footfalls, Raphael felt it could most likely be a man. He leaned unnecessarily against the wall and peeked out into the hallway. He was right. It was a man. It was the security guard from downstairs. Raphael was just about to step into the hall and announce himself when the guard pulled out his pistol and slowed his pace before the doorway to the coffee room. Raphael stepped back inside the door and watched as the guard clearly was sneaking up to the doorway. At the door to the break room, he spun to face inside it with his weapon held meaningfully out in front of him. Then as Raphael moved farther back into the room, the guard turned and said, "There's no one in here," to someone who was walking down the hall from the same direction the guard had come. Again, Raphael thought he might announce himself to keep from being shot by accident, but again he hesitated.

"He left." It was a woman's voice, a voice he thought he recognized, but she hadn't said enough for him to place. He stepped farther back into Gold's cubicle and decided to hide. There was an unattached coat closet, so he slid inside and closed the door softly. He heard the two stop for a second at the office. He supposed they had looked inside the cubicle before the steps continued all the way to the elevator. He heard the doors open and close and then the hum of the elevator car heading down through the building. Hurriedly, Raphael turned off the computer and left the building by the stairs. He didn't feel safe until he reached the street.

He stopped at Morgan's home, but she was not there, and he decided he would eat at his home today rather than eating out. He didn't want to be around strangers at the moment. As he opened the door to his apartment, he was surprised to find Morgan sitting at his kitchen table.

"Can I stay here?" she asked. "I'm worried."

"Sure," he said, relieved she would be with him.

# Chapter Nine

*Jesus said, "Look, the sower went out, took a handful (of seeds),
and scattered (them). Some fell on the road, and the birds came
and gathered them. Others fell on rock, and they didn't take root
in the soil and didn't produce heads of grain. Others fell on thorns,
and they choked the seeds and worms ate them. And others fell on
good soil, and it produced a good crop: it yielded sixty per measure
and one hundred twenty per measure."*

*– the Holy Bible, Catholic Edition*

Raphael and Morgan talked nearly the whole night. He told her everything he knew about what Gold was guessing at. She agreed something strange was going on, and they decided they would find out what they could. They had only themselves to rely on; there was no police force in the city, and no organization that could help them. They went to bed; Morgan on the bed, Raphael on the couch, and in the morning, when Raphael was looking out the window, he saw the suspenders and Derby hat man leaning out from a doorway in the building across the street and peering up at his window. Raphael couldn't make out the man's face and realized the vantage point was too far up for anyone on the street to see much inside his windows, but he was curious why this person who had followed him home the night he spent at Morgan's was outside his building now.

"Come on," he said, jostling Morgan's shoulder. "We have work to do."

After a quick breakfast, they made their way to the office. Walking into the break room, Raphael asked Morgan, "Is it possible to transmit from one place to another without any connection?"

They heard a laugh from the corner. It was Carleen. They hadn't noticed when they had entered, but Carleen was again looking out the window in the corner. "Of course it is," Carleen answered. "All our computers are connected by WiFi. There's no connection there other than an electrical signal. Your TV remote does it by infrared. There are a few ways it can be done. Why?"

"Just curious," Raphael said. "Could it be done with, say, a human?"

"Sure. I suppose. If there was some power source and something that would receive a signal. Sure, it could be done."

"Interesting," Raphael said, looking at Morgan. He peered purposefully into the eyes of his friend, an inquiring look as he nodded toward Carleen, a woman who was known for her prowess with electrical devices.

"Carleen?" Morgan said as she poured her coffee. "I could use your help on something."

"Sure, what do you need?"

"I need to know if our televisions could be transmitting a signal."

"Signal to what?"

"Not to what, to whom."

"To a human?" Carleen asked, her tone surprised. "You mean like some kind of wireless telepathy?"

"Right."

"We should tell her," Raphael said to Morgan. "She should know before we get her into this."

Morgan nodded decisively. "You're right." Turning to Carleen, she said, "Grab your coffee and come to my office."

# CHAPTER TEN

*Jesus said, "I have cast fire upon the world, and look, I'm guarding
it until it blazes."*

*– The Gospel of Thomas, Nag Hammadi scriptures, Codex II*

Carleen, Morgan, and Raphael headed for Morgan's office. As they walked by Will Worton's desk, Worton noticed them for a second and then returned to doing his job, minding his own business, and glancing across the room to Trudy's cubicle. Suddenly, he grabbed his full cup of coffee and dumped it into his wastebasket and slowly headed for the coffee room. His walk would take him directly past Morgan's office door. As the three sat and began to talk, Worton stopped outside the door and listened. He backed up a few steps, leaned against the wall where he could both listen to them and watch Trudy as she worked at her desk about thirty feet away. She hadn't noticed him, and if anyone asked, he was just on his way to get coffee. Worton had no idea who sent him the envelope of money every month with the instructions to "watch over and protect" Trudy. He didn't care. She had a rich father or a benefactor. It didn't matter. The money was welcomed, and he did his job as guard, even though Trudy seemed to loathe the sight of him. He turned back to listening to the conversation in Morgan's office. "Carleen," Morgan started. She looked at Raphael for a second and then said it for the first time. "We think Barry Gold might have been killed."

Worton listened intently as Morgan explained it all; Tafari, silicon dioxide, radio frequencies, the rules, and then she arrived at the point of the meeting. "We need you to help us understand if a message transmitted through the television could be received inside a human being."

"Well," Carleen began, then paused. "How is this going to be dangerous?"

"We got most of what we know off of Gold's computer. Raphael thinks—well, we both think Barry was killed so he wouldn't tell anyone what he found."

Carleen combed back her short black hair with her fingers and thought for a second. "I liked Barry. I'm sorry this happened. You know, it isn't much of a stretch to think the televisions could have a WiFi-type device in them that could transmit a signal, but a receiver inside the body, now that might be a marvel." She stopped and looked at the two. "I guess I would need a TV and someplace where I could take it apart and find out if there is in fact some extra device inside that transmits. That would be the easy part, right?"

Morgan smiled and said, "Right."

Will continued his walk toward Trudy's cubicle with his empty coffee cup. "You alright?" he asked as he passed Trudy. The girl looked up at him but didn't answer.

"I just had mine replaced," Raphael said. "I don't think I could have another replaced, and it didn't take any time for them to replace it at all."

"Besides," Morgan added, "We can't turn in a TV that has been taken apart." She stopped short. "You have one, an extra one," she said to Raphael.

"I do?" He thought for a moment, then answered his own question. "I do. In storage. Carleen, how would you like to go out to dinner tonight?"

Carleen looked quizzically at Raphael at first, but then caught up. "I'd love to, and then maybe we could go back to your place and…"

"Right, we would have all night to work on that TV."

"Morgan, will you be coming?" Carleen asked.

"No, that would be just kinky." They laughed. "We have to keep up the appearance of normalcy, and it seems we are being watched. I don't know who might have killed Gold, but I don't want whoever it was to find out what we're doing."

"So, I'll work on Gold's computer," Raphael recapped. "Carleen will dismantle the television, and you?" He turned to Morgan.

"I have a friend I think we should involve in this situation, if it's alright with you two."

"You mean Trudy? I already have her working in some fact-finding stuff."

"Does she know what you're working on?" Morgan asked, surprised.

"Just that it… well, I guess she does."

"Okay, I'll get together with her," Morgan said, to a face of disapproval from Raphael.

"No, Raphael, really, I need someone to help with this friend of mine, and I don't want to involve any more people other than the ones already involved."

"Except your friend?" he asked.

"Yes." Morgan looked at the two faces who were now staring at her for an explanation. After a pause, Raphael prodded, "So who is it?"

"He's kind of a hermit, a recluse. He had a theory about silicon dioxide back about twenty or twenty-five years ago. Then suddenly he moved up to an island off Newfoundland and hasn't been heard from since."

"And you know him how?" Raphael asked.

"We're half-assed related. Second cousin twice removed or something, but we used to play together when I was a kid. He's brilliant. I just thought he may know something about how a human could receive a radio signal. It is our last link after what you two will be doing. Right?"

"So why do you need Trudy?"

"He, well, he likes pretty girls who are younger than he

is. It might get him to let us visit and open him up to a little bragging."

Raphael smiled. "You're evil," he said to his friend, and they all laughed.

After a moment, Morgan sobered. "It isn't evil to do what needs to be done to correct evil," she said.

# Chapter Eleven

*Jesus said, "What is the kingdom of God like? And to what shall
I compare it? It is like a grain of mustard seed which a man took
and sowed in his garden, and it grew and became a tree, and the
birds of the air made nests in its branches."*

*– Luke, 14:19 – The Holy Bible*

After dinner, Raphael Aronson and Carleen Dumas walked conspicuously to Raphael's house, holding hands. At the doorway she stopped, turned to Raphael, and kissed him. "Just in case someone is watching," she whispered in explanation, then they walked inside. Raphael handed her the key at the elevator and said, "418," then he headed for the storage in the basement to get the discarded TV from years before.

He quickly tugged the smaller Sony from its place tucked between the cardboard boxes of family memorabilia and an old bicycle and boarded the elevator. As it reached the eighteenth floor and he stepped into the hall, he was stunned. Carleen was still standing in the hallway, leaning back against the wall just before his door. Her hands were trembling, and her face was white. On the floor, crumpled in a heap at her feet, was a young man, twenty or so. He was wearing black clothing and black gloves. When Carleen saw Raphael coming, she turned a little toward him. She had a pistol in her hand. "He came out of nowhere," she said. Raphael could now see as he put down the TV that the young man had a knife in his hand. Carleen was crying and between sobs said, "He tried to kill me."

Raphael had reached her and put his hand on her shoulder. "Who is he?"

"I don't know. Raphael, what have you gotten me into?"

"Honestly," he said, "I don't know. Let's get him inside." They both looked around the hall. No one had stepped out of any of the other doors. "Lucky," Raphael said, realizing that all five other residents on the floor had to be out. They each grabbed an arm and pulled the boy inside the apartment. Raphael returned for the TV, placed it on the floor next to the body and locked the door behind him.

"What are we going to do with him?" Carleen asked as she sat down on the couch and stared at the man she had shot lying dead on the living room floor.

"Garbage chute or window," Raphael answered, thinking of how sanitation workers had cleaned up his friend's body. "Our only two options. Can't keep him here."

"If we throw him out of the window, the street cleaners will pick him up in the morning," Carleen said, still staring at the body. "I wonder who he is."

Raphael ruffled through the man's pockets and found absolutely nothing; no wallet, no ID, no money, nothing.

"Are you sure you don't know who he is?" Raphael asked as they slid him toward the window. Carleen shook her head. They edged him to the windowsill, checked the street below for pedestrians, then tipped him out into an eighteen-floor drop. With no police force in the city, the body would be picked up, disposed of, and no one would know who he was or why he had jumped, just like Gold's body had disappeared from the streets the morning after his death.

"I guess we've pissed someone off. I'm sorry I got you into this, but now I think we had better get to the bottom of it before they send someone else," Raphael said.

Carleen nodded her agreement, sat down on the floor next to the TV, and began disassembling it. Raphael took her cue, plugged in the flash drive from his friend's computer, and began opening folder after folder.

He clicked open a file that had no name on it, it was simply labeled "there is." Inside was a grocery list from weeks ago, but at the end it said, "there is an underground trying to topple the Republic."

"Damn," Raphael said and showed it to Carleen.

"I had heard this, but I thought it was just a rumor," Carleen said. "What the hell did Barry find here? And who did he get it from? I guess the big question is who is doing what, and who should we be fighting with and against?" She stopped talking for a moment, then shook her head. "For my money, I would expect the Republic is the enemy, and this underground is who we should be trying to contact." She paused again for a few seconds. "I don't know what he's found, but I found something." She edged the partially disassembled TV toward Raphael and turned the television on its short side.

"You see this purple cross here?" Carleen pointed to the device with the tiny screwdriver she had been using while holding a magnifying glass over the piece she was showing to Raphael. "This doesn't belong in a television. It looks like something I saw in an electronics lab at Columbia when I was there."

"What is it? Wait, I didn't know you went to Columbia. It wasn't in your resume."

"Why are you reading my resume?"

"I don't know. I think when you were hired, Morgan was having me do some of her extra work, like resume reading."

"I don't make a big deal of it. I'm pretty good at keeping a secret. If I remember right, it was a device based on a nanomechanical system. I think it's made out of graphene. It is super thin. I don't see why it couldn't be used to transmit a signal."

Raphael looked at her blankly.

"It's an FM radio transmitter," Carleen explained. "They discovered them back in, I don't know, maybe 2012 or so. At the time, it was supposedly the smallest transmitter associated with wireless technology. Even back then they used it with music signals and then received them on a standard Frequency Modulated receiver. They used them to make very, very thin mobile phones…" They both paused, then Raphael broke the silence to ask out loud what they had both been thinking.

"Do you think it might have something to do with the destruction of all the mobile phones? From what I've heard, those things were incredibly convenient and even more popular," Raphael asked.

"If they are using it for a low power wireless transmission, the phones might have created some kind of interference. Could be," Carleen agreed. "Raphael," she questioned, sitting back against the wall, "What do you think they are transmitting, and who is doing it?"

He took a breath and sat back too. "I guess it would have to be the Republic. I think you're right. The Republic runs the electric company, and that's who brings us the TVs. I always thought it was strange that they pretty much give them away. I mean, other than that piddly little fee we pay every quarter."

"This isn't the first time they gave them away," Carleen offered. "Back in the 1950s, television broadcasting networks realized the real money in TV would be in advertising, making people buy stuff advertised on the tube, and they went throughout the rural Midwest and gave away televisions and even hooked them up for people. What would they be sending now?"

"The rules, for one thing," Raphael said assuredly. "Gold

asked me when I learned the rules, and I have no idea." He turned to Carleen. "Do you?"

"No."

"Shouldn't we try to stop them then?" she asked, sliding along the floor until she was sitting next to Raphael, both with their backs against the wall. Raphael could understand her determination but wasn't sure stopping them was the right thing to do. He wasn't sure yet which side he was on.

"I don't know," he said. "The rules have always worked for me, and whatever they are sending to the world has been working pretty well for most of my life."

"Except for all the damn wars," Carleen added. "And, of course, that small thing that we are possibly being brainwashed by a TV."

"I suppose you're right," he agreed halfheartedly, "but then again, I'm too old for the draft so...." He focused his eyes back on the file from Gold's laptop and saw the top of a photograph; just the top of someone's head full of jet-black hair. He leaned forward and scrolled the picture up. They both look at it silently for a few seconds, then Raphael turned to Carleen and asked, "What's that?"

"It's a picture of me," Carleen answered, her face reflecting her confusion.

"I can see that," Raphael said and scrolled up a little farther. "Beneath the picture are the words 'How do you like it this way?' What's that mean?"

"We used to date," Carleen explained with a smile. "Quite

a while ago, and only a few dates."

"What does that mean on the bottom?"

"My hair cut," she said. "Remember when I cut it? What was it four, five years ago?" Carleen bent over and looked closer at the picture. "He saved that? I'm flattered."

Then a few lines further down was another line.

"Raphael, don't be so trusting. Especially the Associates."

"That's strange," said Carleen. "I thought *he* was an Associate."

"No, a Member. I wonder what he means. I don't even know any Associates. This is bad. If we tell anyone, we'll have to tell a lot of people, or we'll be in this alone, which I feel will be pretty—well, we'll get killed. It doesn't even matter if we agree with what they are sending. If they don't want us to know what it is, we're in danger."

"What are we going to tell them?" Carleen asked. "And who are we going to tell? If we tell everyone, we'll be telling the people who we don't want to know what we have here. I mean, shouldn't we find out who the enemy is first?" This had initially been Raphael's thought exactly.

"You're right," Raphael agreed, "and what do we say? Stay away from the TV, grow your own food, only eat foods that don't have silicon dioxide in them… but what is their goal? What are they trying to make us do?"

Carleen stood up. "I know someone who could tell us."

"Who?"

"The same person who told Gold."

"Tafari. You're right, but we have to be careful to find out what she knows without telling her what we know."

Raphael and Carleen started toward the elevator when the smell of a man's cologne stopped them. "It could be the guy you shot," Raphael offered.

"I know that smell," Carleen said. "It's Eau Sauvage. It's French, real expensive. I used to buy it for my father. I doubt if that kid was wearing it. I don't feel like taking the chance." She reached back for her gun while pulling Raphael at the same time toward the outside fire escape.

They hustled down the outside of the building in the near pitch darkness, feeling their way by clutching the railing. At the street level, Raphael took Carleen's hand and led her down the center of the street. "Not out here," she said and pulled him closer to the side, staying in the shadows. The sound of a skateboard seemed to be following them in short bursts. They stopped and backed farther into the darkness behind the side of a building and waited. The figure was black and rolling along the center of the road, veering right then left, then the young man stopped again almost right beside them. He was drunk and having a difficult time on the skateboard but did not seem to be an immediate danger to them. They let him pass and then continued toward Tafari's apartment. Raphael knocked, waited, then knocked again. There was a rustling inside the door, and then it opened. Tafari was half dressed. She only saw Aronson since Carleen stood back in the darkness.

"Raphael Aronson?" Tafari appeared to be genuinely

surprised. "What are you doing here in the middle of the night?"

"I'm sorry to bother you Tafari, but I have some questions about Barry Gold's death."

"Death? Barry's dead?"

"Oh, come on," Carleen snapped, stepping out of the alleyway and into the light from the door. "You know he's dead."

Tafari stiffened. "Who are you?"

"This is Carleen Dumas; she works with me. She's helping us. We're trying to find out what happened to our friend. You told him a lot of things, and I just had a few questions. Can we come in?"

Tafari backed away from the door and eyed Carleen with suspicion as they stepped inside.

The apartment was pretty much as it had been at their last meeting, but only one lamp was on and the light in the room was subdued. Tafari was wearing shorts and a halter top, and she stopped a few feet inside the room to let the two know they were not going to be staying long.

"Tafari," Raphael asked, "what are they transmitting? We found out even more than you told Gold. We know about the transmitters installed in the televisions. We know someone is transmitting to us, but what is the goal?"

Tafari looked almost relieved. "Is that all? I talk a lot when I'm drunk. I make up stories. Is Barry really dead?"

"You know he's dead, Tafari," said Raphael gently. "I have

the picture he took of you the night he died."

"What? The only picture we ever took was a selfie. Right here on my couch."

"I saw the picture of you across the street in the alleyway the night he died. He took it from his window. I've seen it."

"I didn't kill him. I just found out he is dead. I liked Barry. We were even planning a trip together."

"You told us something the other night about the island of Lesbos. I was wondering what you would know about a picture of it on Gold's computer," Raphael asked.

Tafari moved backwards a few steps deeper into the apartment, and Raphael followed her, but Carleen stepped back toward the door. She was aware that Raphael had done exactly what they had decided not to do. He had told Tafari what they knew before she had answered any of their questions.

"Yes, when I was there with my father, we slept in a beautiful tropical forest on the northwest side of the island. I never forgot it."

Raphael saw a problem in that her description of a forest in bloom was not even close to Gold's petrified forest screen saver, but he decided to let it slide and get more answers.

"Why do you turn off the TV? The rules say we aren't supposed to," Raphael asked, hoping to surprise her.

"I don't know. Privacy?"

"Oh, that's enough," Carleen spit out. "Who is doing the transmitting and what is their goal?"

Tafari suddenly steeled. She put a hand on Raphael's chest

and said, "Out." Simultaneously she knocked on the wall beside her. "Raphael, you're okay, but this one is out." Carleen took a step toward the girl, but a noise behind her stopped her and made her turn. The young man from the sandwich truck was standing behind her and Aronson with a shotgun in his hand. "Problems, Tafari?" he asked.

"No, sorry I called. These two were just on their way out. Would you help them get to the street?"

The young man nodded, and Raphael and Carleen walked in front of him to the street. As they began their trek back, the man surprised them by speaking up and said, "No offense, Mr. Aronson, but you can't come here in the middle of the night and bother my princess. I sort of protect her. It's my job."

"Who is she?" Raphael asked.

"I don't really know, but a very rich man gave me a lot of money to watch over her, so I do. She's a nice kid. I would have killed you if she asked me to."

"Did she ask you to kill Barry Gold?" Carleen asked.

"Barry Gold is her boyfriend, and no, I didn't kill him. I think you already know that. You two should get moving."

The two made it back to Raphael's apartment in the darkness, once again working to not be seen.

"I think we should get some sleep," Raphael said. Exhausted from the events of the night, they disrobed and climbed into his bed.

"The body's gone from the alley," Carleen said as the two lay together in the bed in the darkness. "I know, I saw,"

Raphael answered. It then occurred to Raphael that Carleen had had a hard night. He was truly impressed at her instincts in a crisis but could tell there was something weighing heavy on her now, and it was just in his nature to care about other people before himself.

"She was lying," Raphael said.

"How do you know?"

"Because the forest on Gold's screen saver is a petrified forest. If she saw it in bloom, it would have to be thousands of years ago. She's lying."

He turned to Carleen. "You okay?"

"No, not really," she said, and rolled to him and they embraced.

That is how they woke up the next morning, with a knock at the door.

# CHAPTER TWELVE

*Mary said to Jesus, "What are your disciples like?" He said, "They are like little children living in a field that is not theirs. When the owners of the field come, they will say, 'Give us back our field.' They take off their clothes in front of them in order to give it back to them, and they return their field to them. For this reason I say, if the owners of a house know that a thief is coming, they will be on guard before the thief arrives and will not let the thief break into their house (their domain) and steal their possessions."*

*– Book of Thomas, Nag Hammadi, Codex II*

Morgan Baez was pounding on his door, anxious for any new information from the two. As she began to interrogate them, Raphael hushed her with a look. "It's such a great day for a walk, I thought we might have breakfast to go."

He handed them each a cup of coffee and a USR donut and ushered them out the door.

"We turned the TV off last night, but it's back on now, and I'm not sure the thing is just sending. It might be receiving, too. So, I thought we could better talk outside on the way to work."

"So, you found a transmitter in the TV?" Morgan asked.

"We did," affirmed Raphael, "and it is tiny. I never would have found it, but Carleen did."

Morgan nodded her appreciation to her co-worker. "We know someone is transmitting, but we don't know what, and we don't know why. How do we find that out?"

"We rig a receiver and receive whatever it is they are sending," Carleen offered.

"How do we do that? Do you know how to put it together?" Raphael asked Carleen.

"No, but I know someone who might. He owns a radio and game shop in the Entitleds zone. I could go see him tonight," she said.

"Why not now?" Morgan asked, stopping dead in her tracks.

"Work?" Carleen asked. "I mean, don't we have to work?"

"I think I'm in charge," Morgan said and laughed.

"Okay," Carleen said hesitantly.

The three turned and headed away from work and toward the Classic & Retro Videoshop on the outskirts of the city. Raphael watched as the bars and adult shops became scarce, and then the grocery stores, water stops, and bike shops took over and then disappeared, and after a few blocks of dilapidated single-family homes, he stopped. "Where the hell is this place?" he asked, looking around. "How can he sell anything to anyone way out here? Look at that. There's a pay phone. I didn't think they survived the cell phone. Thought they were all gone."

"It's not far," Carleen offered mildly.

"How do you know this guy?" Morgan asked.

"He was once in the president's cabinet. I picked him for Secretary of Transportation."

There was an awkward silence, and then they all laughed.

"Are you telling me that an Entitled was a cabinet member?" Morgan asked.

Carleen just shrugged and smiled. "Do you really think that is the worst that could happen to positions of power?" Carleen asked, then added, "It's right up here."

The shop was an old gas station/convenience store, and as they stood together inside the door Carleen stepped on a black rubber hose that had been laid across inside the entryway, and a bell rang in the back room. A man about the age of Raphael, or a few years his senior, stepped from the back room. He had what had been called many years prior a Mohawk haircut. His jean shirt was completely open in the front, and he was wearing a beaded necklace. His jeans and sandals were reminiscent of the end of the twentieth century. Morgan and Carleen exchanged glances. "How the hell did you get him by me?" Morgan asked quietly, and they both smiled.

"Can I help you," he began, and then recognizing one of his

customers, he beamed. "Carleen Dumas herself, to what do I owe this honor?"

Carleen seemed a little nervous and quickly introduced the other two, and stepping closer to the man, she said, "We need a little favor."

"Anything for you, Cara mia," the man said, leading the trio deeper inside the store.

"Do you have a television here?"

"I do."

"One of the USR TVs," Raphael added.

"I do."

"We need you to find out what it's transmitting," Morgan spurted.

He stopped smiling and looked at Carleen. She nodded. The man motioned them to follow him into the back room. The room was retrofitted with everything possible that he could find from the period for which he was dressed. "I like the 1970s," he admitted as they all sat on huge pillow chairs that were tossed in a circle around an octagonal slate and oaken coffee table. In the center of the table was a chianti-bottle candle and a cherry-wood jewelry box that was open and displaying what must have been a hundred marijuana joints. He noticed Morgan looking at the box and offered, "They're not real." He reached over and closed the box top.

"So, where is the television?" Morgan asked.

"I don't need one. I already know what is being transmitted. I've known some of it for months, some for years, and some of it only a few weeks, but I know."

"And," Raphael prodded.

The man looked again at Carleen, who nodded for him to go ahead.

"Excuse me," Morgan broke in. "It was a long walk. Do you have a ladies' room?"

"Sure. It's in the back." He pointed out the back door of the room into a small hallway. "Down the hall on the left." Morgan left quickly.

"We found a list of numbers quite a while ago and started trying to decipher them, then about a month ago we found what they were. They were from the Gospel of Thomas, a Gnostic gospel found at Nag Hamadi, Egypt near the Nile River. They were texts hidden in the fourth century. The numbers being transmitted a few every day on the TVs are the numbers of the verses from the Gospel of Thomas."

"Is that it? Bible verses?" Raphael questioned.

"Not Bible verses, Gnostic verses. They never made it into the Bible. They were found in 1945. Most of them are about seeds being planted and some of them grew and some of them didn't. There are some about the kingdom of heaven being inside us, and it seems that it wasn't God who planted all of them."

"Okay, what else?" Morgan asked as she returned to the room. She looked at Raphael and said, "We can look this up ourselves. These books aren't so secret anymore." She turned back to the shop owner and asked, "What else do you know?"

He looked at Carleen again, and she again nodded. "Well, there are other sayings such as, 'The seeds sown are to be harvested.' And 'Similarity breeds contentment.'"

"Damn," Raphael cut in. "That saying comes to my mind all the time." A thought entered his mind uninvited. *"We have to leave,"* it said, but he ignored it. This information was too important.

"Right," the shop owner agreed, "Me too. It isn't by coincidence. It is being transmitted almost every day through the TV. We picked it up on an old army FM receiver that we had someone fit with a printout capability."

The plural pronoun wasn't wasted on Morgan.

"There are others. 'Don't be paranoid,' and 'Everything is always normal' and 'Continue to pray,' and 'What is true for the goose is…'"

"True for the gander," Raphael answered and looked at Morgan.

"Right," the man said, "So you have them too."

Morgan stood up. "We have to leave," she said urgently.

"Thank you," Carleen said.

"Will we see you again?" he asked her.

"No," Morgan answered with finality.

Although Raphael protested and wanted to hear more from the shop owner, he was outnumbered.

"Come on." Morgan hustled him to follow Carleen from the store.

"Why did we have to leave?" Raphael asked.

"We got what we came for. We now know it is being transmitted, and we know what is being transmitted. Now we just have to find out who and why," Morgan said.

"Right," echoed Carleen, "and he didn't know those answers, or he would have led with them."

Raphael looked around the empty streets they were on. "Where the hell are we?" he asked, having become totally lost.

"We're okay," said Carleen.

"Take a right here around this brick thing," Morgan said.

At the corner, with a side street that took a right-angle turn, was a brick structure, enclosed on three sides and open facing the road. It was about twenty-five feet long and six to eight feet deep, and there were two long benches running its length.

"It's an old bus stop," Carleen said to Raphael's quizzical expression. "People used to sit here and wait for the city bus. It would pick them up and take them into the city." As they took the corner, an explosion rocked the ground. Heat buffeted them and Raphael was thrown. His ears rang and he could only hear the way one does under water.

"What was that?" he asked in disbelief. He stood, then took a few running steps back toward the shop when he realized it was gone, and in its place was rubble and a cloud of smoke and fire. Carleen stood dumbfounded at the corner of the street.

The three of them were covered in soot but not hurt. Morgan spoke, but it took Raphael a moment to figure out what she was saying. Her words sounded like she was speaking from a great distance away. "What?" he yelled.

"Let's get out of here," Morgan insisted, grabbing her co-worker's arm and pulling her in the other direction. She turned to Raphael, who stood staring at the smoldering space. "Are you just going to stand there? Let's go!"

The trio walked briskly back in the direction of the city, hoping they wouldn't meet anyone on the way.

# Chapter Thirteen

*"Jesus said, 'If the flesh came into being because of spirit, that is a marvel, but if spirit came into being because of the body, that is a marvel of marvels. Yet I marvel at how this great wealth has come to dwell in this poverty.'"*

*– Gospel of Thomas, Nag Hammadi scriptures, Codex II*

Work was mindless. Raphael sat in his cubicle and thought about a strategy for the president he would create, but his thoughts were jumbled. Mid-morning, Morgan appeared beside him with a coffee.

"Thanks," he said, taking it and placing it on the only empty spot on his desk. He looked up at his friend. "What the hell happened?"

"I don't know," Morgan said, absently shaking her head.

"Did we have something to do with that?" Raphael stared into his coffee. He was still shaken by the turn of events.

She continued to shake her head. "Raphael, we have to talk with Tafari again."

He looked up at his friend, uncertain about what she was saying or what else could be done.

Morgan continued, "I told Trudy what's going on; all of it."

Raphael's expression changed to a question mark.

"She asked what was going on, and I figured she has a stake in this, so I told her."

"Okay," Raphael answered vacantly.

"She still wants to help."

"Okay."

"Want to go speak to her during lunch?"

"Okay."

Raphael took a sip of his coffee.

"See you then," she said.

"Morgan, are you sure we should go on with this? More people could get killed."

"What do you think?" she asked.

"I think I should, but I'm tired of people looking at me after every incident like they're saying, 'What the hell have you gotten me into?'"

"You haven't seen that from me, have you?"

"Well, no."

"Or Trudy?"

"No."

"Carleen?"

"A little." He paused. "No, a lot. She just came out and

asked me. Of course, someone attacked her, and she had to shoot him."

Raphael had expected more of a response, but Morgan just said, "See you at lunch," and left.

At the elevator at lunch time, Raphael was mildly surprised to see his boss, Morgan, and the teenage clerk, Trudy, standing together, waiting for him. It was a pleasant day for what had been a hot, early summer, and the three walked slowly down the center of the street toward Tafari's apartment. As they approached the alley, Gold's young friend stepped from the bar at the corner, smiled at Morgan and Trudy, took Raphael's arm, and ushered them inside the darkened bar that smelled like spilled beer and air conditioning. Raphael assumed Morgan had called the young girl, and she was expecting them. She walked past the fake potted trees and to the empty bar stools.

"Now, what can I do for you?" she asked as she seated the three at the bar, pulled up a fourth stool, and positioned it facing them.

"We have a few questions," Raphael began.

"Shoot," Tafari answered. After a mild inquiry, she stopped Raphael and said, "Okay, so you found that the TVs have been transmitting rules and platitudes, but you don't know why?"

"And we don't know who is transmitting, and if they are just transmitting, or if they are also listening," Raphael added.

"Okay." Tafari shifted, adjusting to be more comfortable in her high-backed bar stool. "Do you want drinks?"

"No," Raphael said. "We need to get back to work. This is our lunch."

"Then leave now, because if you want answers to your questions, it's going to take a bit longer than just lunch." Tafari looked into each set of eyes, waiting for the go ahead. "So, do you want drinks?" She waited a few seconds then raised a hand to the bartender at the other end of the bar. He walked down to where he could hear her. "Three absinthe and pineapple, and one with cranberry juice."

Raphael had a question about the order but kept it to himself.

When the drinks arrived, and the bartender had left their area, Tafari began, "It is the Republic. That's who is transmitting, and yes, they are also amassing a lot of information about all of you."

"By 'you' who do you mean?" Raphael asked as he leaned forward.

"Everyone."

He sat back, stunned. "Everyone? Why?" Raphael pushed.

"For one thing, it's how everyone gets classified into Entitleds, Members, or Associates."

"And the silicon dioxide? You said it was in the food?"

"Right, the food, the water, the beer, especially the beer. I worked putting it in there, so I know this is true. It does what it does. It acts as a catalyst to make the human body a receptor. It doesn't work by itself, but it helps the body receive what is being transmitted by the TV. It is enhanced subliminal perception. You hear the rules and the other things you need to believe at the time. You understand them without hearing them, and you eventually do what they tell you to do. And since the rules are then not something told to you by someone else, but they are your own thoughts, you adhere to them much better than if they were a list like the Ten Commandments." She chuckled.

"How did this happen?" Raphael was half asking and half wondering out loud.

"Well, think back to the history of the mid-twentieth century when the television went from the homes of the very few rich to every living room in the world," Tafari began.

"They gave them away," Trudy suddenly answered, smiling. "It was a beautiful idea. The broadcasters realized the money would not come from the sale of TVs themselves but from the commercials. The more TVs, the more they could charge for the commercials, so they gave away the televisions and reaped the profits. Beautiful."

Tafari nodded and continued. "In the early twenty-first century, when the Republic took over the broadcasting companies, they did the same thing again, only this time it wasn't the commercials that were the end product. Instead, there were shows produced by the Republic; first the news shows, then the entertainment, and then fake shows they made people believe were reality."

Raphael pondered for a short silence and then asserted, "There are no shows produced by the Republic." He wasn't entirely sure of his statement, but he was trying to elicit a response.

"Not anymore," Tafari answered. "After the silicon dioxide built up in humans, shows were no longer needed, and the producers just went directly to subliminally transmitting what they wanted directly to your bodies."

"What is the end goal?" Raphael had finally asked the right question.

"I can't tell you that," Tafari said and hopped down off her stool, pushed it toward the bar, turned to Morgan and smiled, and then walked out into the sunshine. After a few seconds of introspective silence, Morgan caught Raphael's eye and asked, "Do you really want to know the goal? This is getting scary. How bad do we really want to know what is going on?"

"I want to know. Barry is dead, Carleen got attacked, that place we were in blew up, so that guy's dead, and someone is messing with my brain. I want to know."

"Then let's go find out," Morgan said, hopping from her own stool. "It's a road trip. Are you ready?"

"I love road trips," Trudy said excitedly. "Let's go."

"Not so quick." Morgan smiled at the girl's exuberance. "I have to set some things up."

"Like what?" Raphael asked.

"It's a flight and a boat trip, and I would like to see if my crazy cousin wants company. How many should I say are coming?"

"Ummm… four. You, me, Trudy and Carleen, right?"

"Okay." Morgan turned back to the bartender. "Do you have a phone here?"

He turned, picked up a land line phone and brought it down the bar to her. She turned her back on Raphael and began dialing. Raphael took Trudy's cue for a bathroom break, and when he returned, Morgan and Trudy were waiting for him.

"We're all set. We leave in three hours. We just have to pack and get Carleen."

"How long should we pack for?" Raphael asked bewildered.

"I don't know," said Morgan, "better make it a week. We'll meet at the airport in an hour and a half."

# Chapter Fourteen

*"My brain is only a receiver, in the Universe there is a core from which we obtain knowledge, strength and inspiration. I have not penetrated into the secrets of this core, but I know that it exists."*

*– Nikola Tesla*

*"Jesus [said], "One who seeks will find, and for [one who knocks] it will be opened."*

*– The Holy Bible, Catholic Edition*

The airport was crowded almost exclusively with soldiers, so it was easy for Raphael to find the three civilian women. As he walked across the crowded terminal toward them, it occurred to him that he was in the company of three very beautiful ladies. He stopped in front of them, placed his bag on the floor, faced them and said, "Every man in this place is jealous of me right now, and they are all thinking what could

I possibly be doing with the three of you."

The three women looked at each other, and with nearly imperceptible nods they all moved forward at once and while Carleen and Trudy put their arms around him from the sides and Morgan in the middle, Morgan kissed him full on the lips and for long past his point of embarrassment. They stepped away and laughed. "Our plane is waiting," Morgan announced. "Let them wonder."

On the tarmac, nearly hidden by the camouflaged Army transport and the larger bombers, was an antique Learjet 70.

"Is that ours?" Carleen questioned, the wobble in her voice betraying that she verged on the edge of fright.

"It is," Morgan answered with a satisfied smile. "It's a beautiful plane, and it will get us where we are going in about an hour and a half to two hours."

"Where are we going?" Raphael asked.

"Halifax, Nova Scotia." Morgan didn't even hesitate to watch for a reaction but just began walking purposefully toward the stairs leading into the cabin and on into the passenger section. For an antique, the plane was clean and comfortable, with gray carpeting and white plastic and cushioned seats. Raphael took a seat across from Carleen, and Trudy and Morgan faced each other beside them. There were expressions of fright and hesitation exchanged as the jet engines whined to a start.

"Wow, this is pretty nice," Carleen said.

"Glad you like it," Trudy said.

A young woman entered the cabin, pleasantly picked up

their bags and brought them to the back of the plane where she stored them. She returned to the passenger section with blankets and pillows for each of the four people. "Have a nice trip," she said. "We'll be departing in about ten minutes. We will be in Halifax at about 5:45 p.m."

"Not a short trip," Carleen wondered out loud.

"There is an hour's difference between here and there. They are an hour ahead of us, so that means it is about an hour and a half to an hour and forty-five minutes. Not too long."

"Oh," Carleen answered and pulled the blanket up to her chin, tucked the pillow behind her head and closed her eyes. The others also got comfortable, and within ten minutes, the plane taxied to the runway and took off, headed for Halifax, Nova Scotia. Raphael awoke as the landing gear hit the runway on arrival. The others were already awake and looking out the windows.

"We have to hurry," Morgan announced. "We have to catch a boat."

"A boat? Why not just fly there?" Raphael asked.

"Where we are going, the wind most of the time hits about 140 to 200 kilometers an hour gusts, and there is usually heavy fog, so it is less of a danger to take the boat," Morgan answered.

"Oh," Raphael said, almost successfully sublimating the thought of 85 miles per hour winds.

"Less danger, except for the icebergs." Morgan tussled her friend's hair. "My cousin likes it there. It isn't part of the USR. It is part of France."

"I had the strangest dream," Raphael said to Morgan as he sat up and began tucking in the back of his shirt.

"Really, what about?" she asked.

"It had to do with something that happened at that terminal… you know, about the four of us?"

He thought he saw Morgan blush. She didn't tease him. She just smiled up at him as she put her shoes back on.

"Can we get something to eat before we leave? I'm starved," Carleen pleaded.

"Oh, don't worry. They'll feed us on the boat. Most likely more than once," Morgan answered in a matter-of-fact tone. This woke Raphael up a little.

"How long a trip is this?" he asked.

"Twenty-three to twenty-six hours," Morgan answered, as if she had just said a few minutes. "We're going to St. John's Island in Newfoundland. It is the eastern-most part of the North American Continent."

Raphael was pleasantly surprised when he stepped from the airport taxi and saw that the boat was not a trawler as he had feared but a fairly new 118-foot yacht. There was a kitchen and plenty of room for each of them to have a bedroom, which is where they each headed immediately to unpack what they needed for the next day at sea. A few minutes after Raphael finished unpacking, Morgan knocked on his open door. He turned toward her and admonished, "You could have told me."

"Didn't want to scare you," she answered sheepishly. "Would you have come?"

He thought for a minute. "Sure. I guess. What do we do now?"

"The young lady says we will be able to eat in about an hour and that the bar is open now. Or we could get some sun. It's about eighty degrees and no clouds. Of course, it's dark, but…"

"Bar it is," Raphael answered. "Let's go."

The four drank themselves tired, and then they had dinner with wine and went to sleep early. The trip was uneventful and calmly beautiful, and before they knew it, they were finishing their fourth meal, and the young attendant was telling them they were about to enter St. John Harbor, and if they went out to the deck, they would see some whales. Instead, they all went back to their rooms to pack.

Morgan arrived at Raphael's door again.

"I want to show you something," she said and motioned him to follow her to the deck.

On the deck, Raphael saw that they were entering a narrow straight with plush green land on both sides. The straight emptied into a harbor. On the right side was a steep mountain.

"Look up there," Morgan said, pointing to the very top. Aronson had to duck so the top of the deck wouldn't cover where he was trying to see. On the very top of the mountain was what looked to be an old fort. It was small for a three-story building but solidly made of granite blocks. It consisted of a square building with a main house and perhaps three rooms on each of the two main stories, Raphael estimated. It seemed attached to a three-story round sort of granite parapet with a flag on top—an old Canadian flag. From the distance, from the boat, up the mountain, the building looked very small.

"That's where we're going." Morgan said.

Raphael peered at the mountain and for the life of him couldn't establish that there was a road. "You gotta be shitting me. We have to walk that?"

"If I remember right, it has a paved walkway. It's only a few miles, maybe three." She thought for a minute. "Maybe four. But there are stairs." Again she paused. "About two hundred, I think. Along the edge, if I remember, but then there are chains bolted into the rocks, so the climbing is pretty safe if you hold on and don't look down."

Raphael felt a moment of dizziness. "Damn," he said. "You know how I am with heights, and everyone is in better shape than I am."

"Well, that's the right way to go." She hesitated again, considering the path. "Or we could go the left way. It's a road. And up here, out of the city, we can drive."

"Drive? Drive what?" Raphael looked around, wondering if Morgan had lost it. He didn't see any kind of vehicle.

"I'm not sure, but the last time I was up here, there were cars for rent in the town."

"Cars are illegal, and where the hell would anyone get gas? Can you even drive a car?" They were back by his room now, and he was carrying his bag up to the deck.

"Yes, well sort of. I drove once."

Raphael shook his head as they left his room and headed to

the open air. On deck, they met with Trudy.

"Where is Carleen?" Raphael asked.

"Oh, she had a bit of a rough time with motion sickness," the girl said with a smile. "I think she'll be here in a minute."

"Hopefully she'll be over that soon," Morgan said. "We're ready to dock."

"Do we have to pay this guy?" Raphael asked as they began their walk toward the dock.

"All done," Morgan answered. Carleen caught up to the three. She seemed very happy to be looking at dry land. Only a few yards from where they stepped off the boat, a young man was waiting, leaning against an antique automobile. The sleek sedan seemed out of place to those in the group who had never seen one.

"Morgan Baez?" the young man queried, stepping away from the car and toward them.

"Yes," she answered, carrying her bag toward the car.

"What is this?" Raphael asked as the four followed the young man to the back of the car.

"It's a Tesla S model. It's a 2036 or 37 around there."

"It's fifty-eight years old and still runs?" Carleen asked in astonishment.

"Right. We don't use it much. Only for visitors, and you are the first in, well, a long time."

"Where do you get the gasoline?" Raphael asked.

"Doesn't use any. It's electric."

With the bags in the back and the four people packed into

seats, the young man began driving toward the road that led up Signal Hill to the Cabot Tower. All of them stared out the car windows, transfixed by the sight of the craggy landscape. "This is a pretty important place," he said.

"Why so?" Carleen asked.

"I'll show you," the driver answered.

The automobile had no trouble heading along the edge of a cliff, up the steep hill that never seemed to stop climbing. Raphael's stomach was in knots, and he was staring with great determination at the dashboard of the car rather than out the window. He did once shoot a glance to the side, and the views of the harbor and the town were striking, but after a short time Raphael opted to close his eyes against the onslaught of height. It appeared that they were arriving when they came to a small, flat tarred lot next to a building, but Morgan pointed up to the right side.

"There's the stairs I told you about," she said. The car swerved left and continued up an even steeper part of the road. Below, fog entered the harbor and obscured the land on the other side. Soon the boy pulled over and pointed to a stone on which there was a metal plaque. "This was moved here only a few years ago," he said. "You might want to read it." No one wanted to get out, but they read it from within the Tesla.

*"This memorial is dedicated by Canadian Marconi Company to the government and people of Newfoundland to commemorate an outstanding event in the history of Newfoundland and a new era in world communication. The first transatlantic wireless signal*

*was received by Guglielmo Marconi on December 12, 1901 on this spot."*

"Pretty impressive, huh?" the driver asked as he accelerated the last short distance to the Cabot Tower.

"Well, this is it. You are expected."

As the car doors were opened, a brisk wind that had picked up speed all the way on its trip from France hit them. Raphael actually closed the door against it and then pushed hard again to open it up and step out. There was a misty chill, and they all pulled their jackets tight and began.

After a short hike up a paved walkway, they arrived at the front door of the parapet part of the building. Morgan opened the door, and they entered into a small room that housed mostly the wooden stairway up the three stories to the roof. The air was warm, the lighting subdued, and there was a curious plastic sheet on the floor. Raphael had barely finished saying, "Problem with dust? This high up?" when from across the room two men entered, smiling. The older one had large almond eyes, long black hair, and a mustache, and Raphael decided he would be the likely candidate to be the one wearing the Eau Sauvage he smelled. He was dressed in black riding boots, tight black pants, and a white shirt with ruffles down the front button line. The other was more contemporary looking with tan pants, brown shoes, a light blue shirt, and short brown hair. The one with the long black hair smiled at Morgan.

"Ah, Morgan," he sighed. "I haven't seen you in too long." He walked across to embrace her. As he did, the other man, who Raphael and Carleen recognized as the young man who was Tafari's shotgun bodyguard, smiled, walked directly past them, turned to face them from behind, Carleen reached behind her own back for her gun as she began to turn, but she was too late. He pulled out a small pistol, placed it against Carleen's temple, and pulled the trigger. She dropped to the floor on the plastic sheet, dead.

Raphael took a step toward the armed man, but the guard immediately put the gun to Morgan's head and said to him, "You should be still."

Raphael turned to the long-haired man. "Are you crazy? Why the hell… Is she dead?" He knelt beside Carleen.

"She is dead," Morgan's cousin said.

"Why?" Raphael blurted, hovering between fright, flight, fight, and panic.

"She is an assassin. She was here to kill me."

Raphael's heart dropped, and he felt cold all over. "Oh Jesus, Morgan, he's insane. You didn't tell me he was insane."

"You are in no danger," the man said to Raphael.

The other two women stood still, emotionless, seemingly in shock.

"Oh great! You kill my friend and then…"

"She wasn't your friend. She killed your friend."

"What? Who? Who did she kill, that kid?"

"No, he was *my* friend. He was at your home to protect you.

She killed your friend Mr. Gold."

"That makes no sense. Damn Morgan, this guy is nuts." He turned back to the man. "Are you going to kill us too?"

"No, as I told you, you are in no danger. We are on your side." He motioned dismissively to the man with the gun who had just killed Carleen, and the man holstered his pistol.

"Show him," their host said to his associate. The younger man rolled Carleen over with his foot to show the .45 holstered behind her back at the waist of her skirt. He took it out and showed it to Raphael.

"The safety is off," he said and tucked the pistol into his belt. Then he stepped to the bags that had just been brought in. He went directly to Carleen's bag and opened it. Under a layer of night clothes was a double-sided knife about eight inches long, another pistol, this one a .38 like Raphael's, and a picture of the man standing in front of Raphael. At the bottom, etched in pen, was the name Tod Berga. Under another layer of clothes was a long red wig, the same color as Tafari's hair.

"Hello Mr. Aronson. I am Tod Berga." The man offered his hand, and Raphael nearly took it when it hit him again that this man had just killed a woman Raphael had slept with only a few days ago and had worked with for a decade.

"Tod Berga," Raphael affirmed. "The richest man in the world, owner of everything. That Tod Berga?"

"Yes, Mr. Aronson, that Tod Berga." With a motion of his hand, the two women followed him into the next room, a living room with couches at right angles and a coffee table laid out with fruit, cheese, and drink.

As they entered the room, Raphael realized no one was holding a gun on anyone, and he was standing by himself watching the young gunman wrap Carleen Dumas' body with the sheet of plastic. He watched the backs of the other three disappear into the next room. Morgan turned to him in the doorway. "Are you coming?" she entreated.

Dumbfounded, he trailed behind his long-time friend, his supervisor. He followed them to the couches, realizing he could just turn and leave if he wanted to. No one was holding him or the other two there. When they were all seated, the long-haired host poured coffee for himself and the others while talking. "I think first we should clear up this matter of Mr. Gold, and then I think a more formal introduction is in order." He passed mugs of coffee around then sat back, sipped his, put it down on the table and began. "Miss Dumas was an assassin for those who would destroy the Republic. You have heard of them, right?"

Raphael could only manage a nod.

He clasped his hands in front of him and leaned forward. "I am the Republic. Her purpose in life was to kill me and mine."

"Wait, you're the Republic?" Raphael looked around the room at each face and then at Berga, his emotions a mix of anger and confusion and a touch of fear.

"Yes. Myself and a few others, my family, and my name is not Tod Berga. That is just an anagram. I call myself Dagobert."

"Oh, the son of the guy on Trudy's ring. The Merovingian?

Old son of a bitch, aren't we?" Raphael was not about to buy this from the man who had just had Carleen killed.

"I don't think my mother would like that description, but sufficiently old, yes. Miss Dumas had been told that your Barry Gold was an Associate. She had the chance, so she killed him. We had tried to get him and bring him here for his safety. He wasn't an Associate, by the way. Just an unfortunate man who heard too much on a drunken night with Tafari and talked too much when he was drinking. When it became evident that he was associating with Tafari, Dumas' suspicions were underlined, and she killed him."

"What's Tafari got to do with this?" Raphael asked, still not believing a word.

"Tafari is my daughter." Dagobert paused to let that set in. From the entryway, Tafari stepped into the room, went to Dagobert, and kissed him on the cheek. She turned and smiled at Raphael. "Hi Raphael," she said sweetly.

"There are other introductions that have to be made. Are you okay, Mr. Aronson? Should we go on? We could stop for dinner?" Raphael remembered how Carleen had been hungry before someone put a bullet through her head, and he lost his appetite.

Tafari smiled and said, "Raphael, we are really on your side."

"Okay, say I buy all this, what are the other introductions? Who else is joining us?"

"No one," said Dagobert. "But you need to be introduced to someone else. Trudy here is really named ReginTrude. She is also my daughter." Dagobert waited for this to set in. Raphael looked at Trudy, who nodded and smiled. "And my wife," the long-haired man added. Raphael waited for the name, but then realized there wasn't to be another name. Trudy was his daughter and his wife.

"Oh, that is just sick. Morgan, what the hell?" His complaint was not as excited this time. It was more of a resignation.

"It's not really so sick," the host said, sipping his coffee again before continuing. "First, she is much older than thirteen, and second, our people have no recessive genes like your people do. It is more like it was in the beginning of your Bible when incest was not considered a poor choice. No recessive genes, no malformed offspring, and malformed offspring are something we have always tried to avoid."

"Then," Raphael began, then stopped and looked at Tafari.

"No," said Berga. "She is not Trudy's daughter. Different marriage. I've had several. Sometimes more than one at the same time. Earth can be a lonely place after a while. Don't think I haven't been chastised for it. It's just a nominal thing, not genetic."

"Wonderful," Raphael said and allowed himself to sip some of his coffee. As he put the cup down on the table, his awareness had returned and he asked, "You said 'our people'. Who are you?"

"That is a question of some difficulty. We are not from this place, but we are from here. This question has been asked previously, and before you can understand the nature of who we are, you will have to understand more about who you are."

"So, you're not going to tell me. Morgan, I have had enough."

"I haven't," she answered. "Just listen. We're here, so what have you got to lose?"

"Okay then," Raphael returned his attention to his host. "Who am I?"

"To answer that, we need food. It is time for dinner." Berga rose and strode into the next room. Raphael looked to his boss, and she laid a hand on his arm. "Let's hear him out. I doubt if we are in any danger. If he wanted to kill us, I'm pretty sure we'd be dead. And unless you are up for running down that hill and swimming home, I think we should wait this out." They followed him and the two young women into the next room, where a dinner table had been set with a small serving of white rice covered with a generous helping of beef burgundy with a few white onions. Raphael couldn't help noticing that his plate and Morgan's also had a helping of asparagus, but the others didn't.

Wine was poured.

"Tell us what happened to Barry Gold," Morgan said after a few bites of the beef and a sip of wine.

Dagobert pushed the plate toward the center of the table and sipped his wine. "My daughter was being called home for a reason," he began. "She tends to go overboard in the ways of humans and especially, as you may have noticed, in the ways of the Entitleds. In short, she drinks too much and talks too much; a family trait, I'm afraid. She met your Barry Gold and was as attracted to him as our men were to your women long ago." He sipped his wine again. "I like wine. It is a wonderful thing. You should look at your Bible. Genesis tells about that foolishness and what it caused, and my young and foolish daughter was making the same mistakes as our ancestors. She told too many things to her new partner that she should not have told him, and he in turn began talking in public about these things. This put him in danger. He put some of this information on his computer, which of course you found." He nodded at Raphael, then continued, "Your friend was in danger when Carleen Dumas found out about what information he and Tafari were discussing. Dumas must have found out who Tafari is and then assumed Gold was one of my Associates. He wasn't. I sent for Tafari Alexandria and told her to come here and to bring Mr. Gold with her. But it was too late. Wearing the red wig you saw in her bag, Dumas followed him home from my daughter's apartment. He managed to get a picture of her, not understanding why Tafari would have followed him home. Of course, when he opened the door, he was killed and dumped out the window into the alleyway."

"But he called me and told me *a man* had followed him." Raphael questioned.

"A man did. But only to ascertain the address. When Mr. Gold saw him, he must have called you, but when he looked again, the man was gone, and Dumas was already on her way.

You met him once."

"When did I meet him?"

"He owned the shop you were taken to by Dumas. He was a man we had been trying to find for a while. He was a terrorist from the group that had been plotting to destroy the Republic. I would like to say it had never happened before, but that would be a lie. We found him, so we stopped him." Dagobert paused. "Did you dispose of his body, Mr. Aronson?"

"What? No."

Raphael thought back to all the things that now made sense. He sipped his wine and began to eat. He thought about the fact that it had been Carleen who told him the enemy must be the Republic. He focused on the photograph on Gold's computer, her studies at Columbia that never made it to her resume, her anger with the wars, Gold's warning, "Raphael, don't be so trusting" coming right below the picture of Dumas, how adamant she was with Tafari. Then there was Tafari's immediate reaction to the inquisition. He decided it could possibly be true that Carleen had been playing him, that she could in fact be an assassin.

"Okay," Raphael said calmly, quietly, "Suppose I believe this about Carleen, what is it I need to know about myself before I find out who you are?"

"Not you, Mr. Aronson." The answer came surprisingly from his right instead of from his host, who was directly across from him. Trudy had answered. "About all of you. You need to know your history."

Dagobert wiped his lips daintily with a linen napkin, even though Raphael hadn't seen him eat a thing. "We, our kind, arrived first about two million years ago and found a thriving planet, lush with plants, fed by abundant water, and several types of animals, birds, fish, and a strange little creature we thought could be bred and made to colonize the planet and make it a perfect place to live, for us. We are spirit that became matter, as opposed to you who are matter that became spirit."

Raphael, at the edge of his will to believe, jumped on the preposterous assertion. "Are you saying humans weren't as good as you, so they had to be wiped out so you could colonize earth? Is that what you've got? Some B-rate horror movie from the last century? This is what you want me to believe?"

The eyes of the long-haired man flashed at Raphael's accusation. "If you have ears, you should listen. If you seek, you shall find. If you listen, you will understand. If you understand, you will be astonished and angry, and when you are angry, you will rise above the others." As Raphael sat in disbelief, Berga leaned toward him. "It says this in your scriptures. Please Raphael, you have ears. What harm could it do to listen?"

He paused and locked eyes with Raphael before he started again. "No, you weren't meant to be wiped out. Wiped out, what a perfect communication. No, the planet was to be made perfect for us *and* for you. We began our experiment. We used some birds and mice-like creatures and this curious little hairy biped. We enhanced their DNA and then we left. You called this species of your ancestors the Homo Ergaster. It's all in your books. It's all true. We sowed our seed on someone else's land, on God's land, and made you into our image and likeness; or at least closer to our image and likeness. The total process was a long one. We are geneticists. We altered your DNA."

Raphael now dove into his meal like a hungry man. He did not believe any of this foolishness. Morgan's cousin, or whatever he was, was nuts, and so were his two concubines. He stopped eating and looked up from his plate. "Okay," he said, smiling his full disbelief. "Two million years ago your people came here and made humans? Do I have that right?"

Berga grimaced. "No, you don't have it right, and it is important that you understand before we go on. We didn't make humans. We changed your DNA. The ones sent here were geneticists. They didn't create you. They set you on a different path. God created you. We just came later and according to your own Bible 'sowed our seed' on God's land and made you into our image and likeness. Raphael… may I call you Raphael?"

"Sure," he said with a short laugh. "Shit, you can call me whatever you want. You made me in your image and likeness, right?"

"Mr. Aronson, let me explain something that is also in all of your books, something you have overlooked. The god you all worship? The one who stood up and shouted that he was the only god and was to be worshipped by anything else in existence? Your first god, he was a bad god. It is told in our books, and in yours, that he was a serpent with a head like a lion. It wasn't supposed to be your god at all. He was created by accident, and in his consciousness, he was pompous and egotistical. His first words, according to history and scripture, were, 'I am the only God. Thou shalt not have false gods before me.' This evil-god situation was fixed by the real creator, and the second creator god became the God you believe you worship. The second God was all good, and humans put the two together in books only to make it easier for shepherds, farmers, and fishermen to understand."

"So, you're not saying you're God?" Raphael sounded as if he found this a bit surprising.

"No. God created all of this. We don't know God any better than you do, except that God was most likely the first thought, the true creator. The only thing we know for sure that you don't seem to know is that God exists. Well, actually two gods existed."

"Aliens, then?" He took a quick sidelong glance at Morgan to presumably share a laugh, but she wasn't laughing. Dagobert thought for a short time while he motioned for his food to be taken away uneaten. "Not aliens either, not how you understand them, little green men, little gray men and all. We started here. We were created close to here and were first alive on Earth. We just aren't human; not totally, anyway. This doesn't matter yet. Please, don't believe if you do not want to, but hear what I'm saying."

"Okay, so what happened to the little hairy bipeds?"

"We let them grow unattended, as it were. They became

a plethora of different types, but the ones we saw when we returned were the hominids your scientists have begun calling Homo Erectus. We decided that since the genetic changes had worked, environment might be a curious variable to introduce, so we spread them out from Africa where they had begun. We took some to what is now Europe and some to Asia a little more than a million years ago. We were correct. The environment in Africa was perfect for homo erectus, and he grew and flourished. In both of the other places, we decided to help the population. In Europe and Asia, we altered the genetics again. The Europeans evolved again, this time into what you call Neanderthal. Those in Asia moved in a different direction, and you now call them Denisovan. There were several other what you call off-shoots, but these three were the ones who interested us the most."

"What about the missing link?" Raphael asked.

"We are the missing link. We changed you from monkeys to humans. It seems God had a plan, but we screwed it up. Listen to me. About 700,000 years ago, we forced the experiment to progress. We shouldn't have done that. We should have allowed evolution to take its course, but we were impatient. In Europe, what you call Heidelberg man emerged and began to migrate. We hadn't expected this. Heidelberg migrated into the Asian location of the Denisovan, and the two began to interbreed. It watered down the Denisovan genetics a bit but not before some of them migrated into Southeast Asia and then on to what is now New Zealand and Australia, which were one body of land at the time, no ocean separation. But since they had to travel across about sixty-five to seventy miles of open ocean to get to New Zealand, and their boats were only at a stage that made the trip extremely dangerous, we gave them a bit of an assist. This assist is depicted in some of the artistry of the Denisovans in Australia at the time. No one knows what those pictures are, or you won't believe it, but they are us."

"How long are you saying you have been here?" Raphael realized he almost sounded as if he was beginning to believe.

"Mr. Aronson, we do not die. It is one of the biggest differences between us. Another distinction is that we are spirit who has created material, while you are material who has created a soul. You were a marvel, even to Jesus. As your own books explain, 'If the flesh came into being because of spirit, that is a marvel, but if spirit came into being because of the body, that is a marvel of marvels.' Jesus said that. It is written in your own Gospel of Thomas. Anyway, to continue. Denisovan were from that point left out of further experiments. They continued to exist and change and even took some of their Neanderthal genetics with them. This is all in the scriptures, you know. They are just called different things. So now the Denisovan men and women were in parts of Southeast Asia and in Australia. But the truly interesting part is that when we returned about 370,000 years ago with the idea of trying something new, we helped the brains of the two main species to grow larger, even to the point of abstract thought."

"How did you do that? Did you alter the genetics again?"

"Yes, but we also taught them to kill, cook, and eat animals. The rush of protein helped grow their brains. And when we left, we had created two distinctly different species of humans. There were several other types, but these were the ones we spent our time on. The ones in Africa began to evolve toward modern humans, what you call Homo-Sapiens, and the species in Eurasia began evolving toward Neanderthal."

Trudy had heard enough for one sitting. She knew the story well and was becoming bored. "Let's go outside and watch the stars," she said. She looked directly at Raphael and added, "Some people say the stars are angels. You know, like the Watchers. Do you think I could be a star?" Without waiting for an answer, she grabbed the bottle of wine and her glass from the table and left the room.

Outside, the hilltop was windy, but it was warm enough, and in the dark the wind felt comfortable. Leaving the bench open for the women, Raphael and Tod Berga sat down on the stone steps. A graying Irish wolfhound bounded across the grass from the parking lot and, much to Raphael's relief, laid down at Dagobert's feet.

"Then what happened," asked Raphael, who now seem totally engrossed in Dagobert's story even if he wasn't completely convinced of its authenticity.

Dagobert reached down and patted the dog. "We took another peek at Earth about 300,000 years ago. Neanderthals covered what is now Europe, but the real interest was in Africa.

A very strong and capable species had evolved. We couldn't help ourselves when we saw the potential in the Africans, so again, we enhanced their DNA."

"I thought you said that was forbidden," Raphael said, stretching his mind across the black ocean that lay before him all the way to Ireland.

"It was. This change was, well, not really sanctioned, but Neanderthals had progressed much farther than we had expected. This was quite amazing to us. We had decided we might do away with all but one species at this point, but instead we decided to let both species evolve."

"A competition?" Raphael asked.

"Not really. Neanderthals were not a concern of ours. They had progressed only because of the inter-breeding and genetic alterations being passed on to the hybrid offspring. It would die out. We were now focused on the people you called Homo erectus who were on the verge of becoming what we were aiming for; we were grooming them to become what you call Homo-Sapien.

"It was about 125,000 years ago, and when we looked back in, homo erectus was moving around in Africa. We set up shop in several places and began to capture and examine the humans. Evolution was working fine, a perfect natural selection of the fittest. The Africans had begun their migrations toward Europe, and we figured there would eventually be a clash. We decided to allow nature to take its course. We believed the brawn of Neanderthal could not stand against the intelligence of the new breed, and we left.

"At about 40,000 years ago, we returned. What we found was astonishing. The Africans had migrated into Europe, but rather than war, the two types had begun living together. We again dabbled in the genetics of the Africans. This is where your Bible begins. This is where abstract thought began to take over the minds of humans. We were also proud of our progeny that they had drawn our likenesses on cave walls."

"I'm not sure why abstract thought is such a big deal. I mean, are you saying there was no abstract thought before this time? And was it only in humans?" Raphael looked pointedly at the dog at Dagobert's feet. "He obviously has feelings for you. Isn't that abstract thought?"

The angel thought for a few seconds then produced a dog biscuit from his pocket and wagged it in front of the dog, who immediately rose and approached him. When the dog was only a few inches from the biscuit, Dagobert turned to Raphael. "Catch," he said and tossed the food to Raphael. The dog followed it and sat at Raphael's feet. Dagobert smiled. "The difference between love and hunger. The difference between thought and abstract thought, instinct and reasoning."

Dagobert turned to face Raphael. "This was a very important time. It was the most defining change in human beings. We added now what you now call the FoxP2 gene. You had the gene, but at this time we mutated it before we left. We changed positions 911 and 977 of exon 7. We made two alterations in the DNA of the ones you now called Homo-

Sapien. They became the only species who survived as a pure species."

"What happened to the others?" Raphael asked.

"Well, Denisovan were pretty much in Australia and Asia, and we left them there to be observed. The most interesting at the time were the Australians. The hybrid genetics for some reason were evolving nicely, and, although they had about three hundred languages, they could communicate with each other as if they all spoke one language enough so they built trade routes across the continent. This and their interbreeding in a large gene pool let them flourish. They were pretty good travelers. At one point, they were in Mongolia, Australia, Asia, and one of the Hawaiian Islands before the Polynesians arrived. We also found them on a small island off Europe. They were called all kinds of things: Mongols, Menahune, Aborigines, Leprechauns. They were pretty much called the little people almost everywhere they migrated, and they were the only hominids who could communicate non-verbally. It seems they still can."

"Leprechauns?" Raphael nearly spit out his wine. He looked again to Morgan, but she only said, "Go on, we're listening."

"The new changes in Homo-Sapiens would allow them to communicate nonverbally and verbally with each other through thought and language, and most importantly, they now developed abstract thought."

"But we can't do that even now, the nonverbal, one-language communications thing," Raphael protested.

Raphael stood and held up a hand, palm toward Dagobert. "Can you wait just a minute? This is a lot. I mean, it is so much. I need a break." Dagobert nodded regally, and Raphael walked away from the people with thoughts spinning through his head. He walked toward the cliff and let the cool air clear his head. His world had just turned over. He had never associated God with science before, and to believe his host was to believe an entirely different universe. He took a deep breath and returned. The others were still sitting as if Raphael had never left.

As he sat back down, he asked, "We were allowed to communicate nonverbally with you and with each other, but we can't anymore? Is that where we are?"

"True, humans never understood the extent of their own powers, and over time, through non-use, the powers diminished. It shriveled like your appendix. When you didn't need it, it just stopped working, and so did your telepathic gift. This is where they began to leave the lush environs of Africa and spread out in search of what they didn't know."

"Some say that they were tossed out," Aronson tested.

"Whatever makes it easier for you to understand. Abstract thought had given birth to questions such as who are we, where did we come from, where are we going? They learned, with help, to create languages, to tell stories, to work with weapons and tools, create art. They even learned that there was such a thing as good and evil, but they never really knew that they could communicate nonverbally with each other or with us. The ability was stifled through ignorance of its existence and became a form of inexplicable empathy throughout the Middle Ages and the dark ages, and then that too dwindled to nothing somewhere in the late twentieth century."

"Let's walk," Dagobert offered as he stood from the stairs and led the way slowly down the walkway to the edge of the precipice. Raphael and the women followed.

# Chapter Fifteen

*"…that the sons of God saw that the daughters of men were
beautiful; and they took wives for themselves, whomever they
chose. Then the LORD said, 'My Spirit shall not strive with man
forever, because he also is flesh; nevertheless his days shall be one
hundred and twenty years.' The Nephilim were on the earth in
those days, and also afterward, when the sons of God came in to
the daughters of men, and they bore children to them. Those were
the mighty men who were of old, men of renown."*

*– The Holy Bible, Catholic Edition, Genesis 6:3*

As they reached a point where Raphael was getting visibly
nervous with the angel's history lesson, Dagobert offered
a seat on a different stone wall, and they all sat down.

"It is good," Dagobert said as they all got comfortable
as they could on the rocks, "to see the world from different
points of view. For instance, from here you can see the mouth

of the inlet. It is through that inlet that everything exists that keeps those who live on this island alive."

He shifted slightly, and his gaze drew inward. "Anyway, when we returned to see our handiwork, about 35,000 or 40,000 years ago, we had let the Africans grow, and before we knew it, they were coexisting with what was left of the Neanderthals."

"Coexisting?"

He nodded. "Yes, and it wasn't just the Neanderthals. There were others who saw the beauty in humans and mated with them. This was what you call original sin. The two human species had interbred, and a new group had also interfered with the seed of humanity. We hadn't expected that."

Raphael's brow furrowed as he thought. "God?"

"No. They were not God. They were like us, but not us. Visitors have come from eight places. We are one. This group was another. They stumbled onto the Earth and our handiwork. Although they interacted with the Neanderthal, it was the Homo-Sapien that drew most of their interest. For a time, they only watched. We stayed away from them, and they stayed away from us."

"And you both messed with humans." Raphael was getting angry now, partly because he found himself believing the story. How could he not believe? It was all founded in both science and religion. It all made more sense than anything else he'd heard.

"Some of the Homo-Sapien DNA had found its way into

the Neanderthal and sadly, vice versa." Dagobert stopped to let the last words sink in. "There they were, the Neanderthal were making tools, drawing pictures, telling stories, and had begun communicating with each other. This was not our goal at all. We had expected one group to kill off the other. We had been short-circuited. The two species began to co-exist, to interbreed, and Homo-Sapien had passed the new genetics backwards. Sort of sowed their own seed in our garden. The genetics worked both ways, and now we had Neanderthal genes in Homo-Sapien and vice versa. We weren't sure if we were going to start over or not."

"Why would you have to start over? And who the hell are you to decide that?" Raphael asked.

"Believe me, that question was asked, and as strongly as you just asked it. The answer was that the combination of genetics had transformed the Homo-Sapiens into humans who had taken on animal characteristics, and the Neanderthals were animals who had taken on human characteristics. Your own scriptures call it the lion eating man and the man eating the lion. Only one type is good. It was in the Gospel of Thomas. I never understood why your leaders didn't want people to know this. The words go, 'Blessed is the lion that the human will eat, so that the lion becomes human. And cursed is the human that the lion will eat, and the human become lion. I did tell you that the good in humans came from God, and the evil in you came from Yaldabaoth, the serpent with the lion's head, didn't I?"

"Yes, you told me. So how are you and your kind not God?"

Raphael was torn between anger and curiosity.

Dagobert stood up and strolled to the edge of the walkway and looked directly down the cliffside. Then he turned back to Raphael. "God is different. God is what made the stars and planets and the first form of beings and all the animals and plants."

Dagobert caught Raphael's eye and said, "God made us too, and God even created the others who have visited you. But in a way, we are your fathers and mothers. Your gods. We didn't decide that. You did. We changed you into our image and likeness. Then your stories got mixed, and you began to worship us, and the others, and a bad god, and a good God, and well, humans got confused. Forcement, how you say, necessarily confused."

Dagobert looked around the group. The humans, even Morgan, were getting tired. Raphael's eyes were nearly glassed over, and he seemed to Dagobert to be losing interest.

"I think that is enough for tonight. Please, Mr. Aronson, take away from this that we are your friends, and that what I say is at least possibly true. We'll continue tomorrow."

Raphael was struck by intense doubt over everything he had heard. "I don't think so. I don't think any of this is possible." He began to get up from the steps. "You haven't shown me how any of this could be possible. Why the hell would I believe this insane story?"

"You've believed more insane stories without proof, but let me add one more thing," said Dagobert. "In the way of proof." He whispered to Trudy, who smiled and went inside the house.

"What?" Raphael asked. Dagobert held up a finger until Trudy returned with an armful of apples.

"This dessert, this apple."

"Are you going to tell me that is the forbidden fruit?" Raphael mocked, as he received one from Trudy. He immediately put it on the stone step beside himself.

"No. Apples weren't the forbidden fruit at all. It wasn't even a fruit that was forbidden. There were no apples in the Middle East in biblical times, Raphael. You can look it up."

"So, it's a metaphor. We all knew that."

"But you are wrong. It isn't a metaphor or even a fruit. It was a misinterpretation. The word for apple is 'malum' in Latin. The word 'malum' in Latin simultaneously means 'evil.' But the apple in front of you tells something that humans are capable of." Dagobert held out his apple toward Raphael. "In what was the USA long ago, there was only one form of apple. It was the crab apple. Everything else was a crossbreed, done through grafting, selective breeding, or cross-pollination. When your Jefferson was king or president, the king of France sent him a new kind of apple. It was called the Ralls Genet. It was a wonderful apple, but when it was planted, the farmers found out that it would grow best in Ohio, not Virginia, and so that is where it flourished."

"And this is a Ralls Genet?" Raphael was still unimpressed.

"No. The Ralls Genet didn't last in America, but some humans in Japan felt their island needed American apples, so they procured some Ralls Genet from the USA and also procured another apple that had been made to grow fine in America, the Red Delicious apple. The Japanese crossbred the Ralls Genet with the Delicious and created the Fuji apple, which flourished in Japan.

"This is a Fuji, an apple that started as a crab apple and was genetically modified through selective breeding and cross-pollination into several different types of apples. Then two of the hybrids were mated. That effort was moved to an environment more conducive to its proliferation, and it finally became this wonderful fruit you have before you."

"What does that prove?" Raphael asked.

"If you humans can do that with your apples, why would you disbelieve that someone could have done it with you?"

"Because human beings are much more complicated than apples." Raphael tossed the fruit onto the grass and began again to turn away.

"Not genetically," the geneticist said. Raphael stopped. His host continued. "There are 57,000 genes in the genome of an apple. And there are only 30,000 in that of a human. I'll let you take that to bed with you. We'll talk again tomorrow. And, by the way, your scientists have only deciphered about five percent of it, and wrongly call the rest 'junk.' Think about it."

Raphael picked up the apple, looked at it thoughtfully, and returned to his bedroom.

# Chapter Sixteen



*Jesus said, "When you see your likeness, you are happy. But when you see your images that came into being before you and that neither die nor become visible, how much you will have to bear!"*

*– Gospel of Thomas, Nag Hammadi, Codex II*

In the morning, Raphael walked quietly from his room, down the colorfully painted purple and white wooden steps, crossed the entryway, and stepped outside into a comfortable seventy-degree day. He pulled his sport coat tight against the mountain-top wind, smelled the salt air, walked out to the front, and sat on a rock overlooking the harbor to the right and the open ocean to the left. He had convinced himself during the night that Carleen Dumas could possibly, and even probably, be exactly who Tod Berga said she was, but he still couldn't dismiss the violence of her death carried out right in front of him. He knew that the history of the human race that he had heard over dinner was pretty much accurate: the dates, the geography, the different species of humans. He had decided somewhere around three in the morning that it didn't matter whether it was God's hand or evolution or both, or if it was the story told by his host of genetic manipulation by some otherworldly species that brought humanity to its current place. It pretty much started out where Dagobert had said it started, and according to science, history, and even the religious history in the scriptures, it progressed pretty much the same way he said it had. Raphael did ponder that, in his knowledge of the progress of mankind, it had never occurred to him that God and science could be the same thing. He remembered something he had heard years before: "God said He did it. He didn't say how."

He was having a problem, however, understanding the dual gods of creation; the ones Berga had said were melded into one in the Bible to make it easier for humans to understand. What had he called the first god, Yaldabaoth? The evil and conceited god with the enormous ego. And the second, the creator; this second one being the real God that most of the world worships under one name or another.

Raphael walked down the steps on the edge of the outer rim and looked out at the ocean far below him, stretching toward the horizon, seemingly forever. He was in awe of the huge barges that looked so little and insignificant from up here as they skirted icebergs in the opening to the harbor.

Suddenly, he realized he had gone too far down the walkway and was hanging desperately onto a chain that was bolted into the rock wall behind him and peering straight down a steep cliff that ended four hundred and seventy feet below in the Atlantic Ocean.

"How the hell did I get here?" he asked out loud. Everything he knew about himself told him not to go here, but this is where he found himself this morning. His instincts and his phobia made him turn his back to the ocean and look directly into the rock only a few inches in front of his face. It was solid, safe. He gripped tightly the one safety device in his reach, the thick hardness of the chain. He gathered himself, adjusted his feet, calmed his breathing and said to the rock, "Raphael Aronson, you fucking coward."

He turned back to the ocean, to the cliff in front of himself. He let go of the chain, took a deep breath, and drank in the cool beauty of what had frightened him a few seconds before. Without the use of the chain, he walked back to the steps that climbed toward his origin, the stone building.

When he entered, the others were already in the dining room and breakfast had been served.

Not everyone turned when he entered the bright sunlit room, but the smile from Morgan settled him a bit. There was a long wooden table covered with a white tablecloth, and he was comforted by the familiar smell of coffee, bacon, and the warm aroma of some kind of incense. His place was being set by the same young man who had killed Carleen. Raphael still had suspicions about him and eyed him with distrust. He waited for the young man to depart the area of his chair before he sat down. He smiled at Morgan.

Tafari spoke first. "Mr. Aronson, I have to tell you, I really liked Barry. I am so sorry that I have a big mouth when I drink."

Instead of answering, he turned to Tod Berga. "Okay, I'm up to speed. Go on."

"Good. Where were we?"

Raphael took a deep breath, ready to listen. "I have been convinced of Carleen's identity, and I have been convinced it is probable that your people had been directing our genetics for a million or so years. There were three types of humans left that you were interested in. Someone else had come while you were gone and messed up your divine plan, and you were deciding whether or not to destroy your spoiled product, us, which obviously you didn't do. But first, I want to know about this first god of the Bible. The one you said was jealous and egotistical and evil. I was never told about this."

Berga leaned back and tented his fingers. "Yes, you were. Jesus told you. You just didn't listen. You were also told in the gospels of Judas, Nicodemus, John. The Book of the Egyptians tells the whole story. Others told you too. It is all throughout your scriptures, but your religious leaders carved him out of existence by tossing out a lot of the early books.

"In a nutshell—I love that saying. En un mot. In a nutshell, beautiful. When Earth was ready to be inhabited, an entity named Sophia was sent here along with the spirit of who you call Jesus the Christ. They were to create a human being, part God, part earthly inhabitant, all good. Sophia, being androgynous, made a mistake. She struck out on her own, and Yaldabaoth was created without the help of Jesus. This god of the chaos, who was born of wisdom without goodness, in turn created humans, and those humans were part good and part Yaldabaoth. God tried to protect the misbred humans and sent angels to take care of them, but the humans had a soul and the angels didn't. The angels who were sent saw the misbred creation that was human, and some of them balked at caring for the humans. While the angels had turned a blind eye to the humans, Yaldabaoth came to Eve in the garden and the rest is history. Well, your history, anyway."

"And we have been worshipping the wrong god ever since?" Raphael said. He had to admit he had thought this to be a possibility his whole life. It was difficult to understand why a good god would promulgate so many wars and sacrifices and murders as appeared in the Old Testament.

"Oh, so you are paying attention, but that is not entirely true. You have been worshipping two masters. Jesus said you shouldn't do that. Anyway, we didn't destroy all of you, correct? We changed the weather a bit and starved out the Neanderthals about 40,000 years ago. The Denisovans almost followed suit, as you say. We expected that they would also be extinguished, but they weren't.

"The ice age that we brought on with a slight tilt of the earth on its axis was sucking up all the moisture in the air and making ice out of it. This froze Europe and killed the vegetation and made the animals migrate. It also dried out nearly the whole continent of Australia. As you know, it is no longer lush. It is now a desert. But unlike the Neanderthal, the Denisovan avoided extinction, which we fully believed they could not avoid. But rather than the gene pool being splintered into three hundred tiny pockets of humanity, which would produce a shallow pool and drive the Denisovans to extinction, this pocket of humanity, all three hundred tiny pockets of them, began to communicate with each other nonverbally across the whole continent even though they spoke hundreds of different languages. With the communication, they were successful in creating trade routes across the deserts and the jungles, and they survived by helping each other and by expanding their own gene pool by three-hundred-fold. It was a quite remarkable feat. So, we let them survive. They were the ancestors of what you call aborigines, who still communicate nonverbally with each other."

"How old are you?" Raphael asked.

"Me, personally? I don't know," Berga answered. "Very old."

"What is your first recollection of Earth?"

The angel seemed to squirm a bit, his face thoughtful as he appeared to consider the question. The first impression he had formed of earth was something he could never forget. It had been formulated for him by his teacher. He was no longer sure, but he thought it had frightened him.

"You wouldn't like it. There were rivers of fire, volcanoes, and vicious lightning. There were clouds of methane, and then there was water that came from the heavens. My kind were born here and then, from fire and light. Several eons later, life began. I only saw that first part in descriptions from elders. The first I saw for myself there was life, blue and green and cooling rain and fresh air. It was a paradise when I first saw it. But back to the answer to who you are.

"This left only you to be administered to, or to be precise, your Homo-Sapiens, to evolve into what you were supposed to be from the beginning, albeit they were carrying the mistakes and aberrations of history, such as the imperfections from the first creation and the mistakes of our own people, as well as the incursion of the others."

"What were we supposed to be?"

"You were supposed to be able to communicate with each other without speaking out loud. Speaking out loud was primarily for singing. And you were supposed to be able to communicate with us, or at least be able to be communicated with by us. And you were supposed to be basically good. Since you were the aberration of good and evil, you were not what you were supposed to be. Well, most of you weren't."

"We were basically evil?"

"No, you were basically good and evil, and you were endowed with free will to choose either."

Dagobert held up the conversation while the young man, who was acting as a server, began refilling coffee cups. Raphael looked at Morgan and found her totally comfortable in the face of what he found to be life shattering. Trudy and Tafari, who had to be bored by a conversation they had probably heard several times before, still smiled and conversed softly with each other in the intermission between parts of Dagobert's explanations.

"It worked pretty well," Dagobert broke the silence as the server left, "but then other outerworlders I told you about had a falling out with each other and some decided Earth was good enough as it was. They came to Earth to live, to rule. I was told there had been some kind of war. It seems our manipulations had drawn the interest of the others. They decided they would return and steal our work to that point, not to enhance the race but to rule it. To make matters worse, the Homo-Sapiens were beginning to look an awful lot like us when we took bodily form. We had made you into the image and likeness of ourselves. These others, who you called fallen angels, found they enjoyed the human women and, well, they changed the DNA again. It messed up what we had been trying to do all along. The women were exceptional, especially the ones with the long, flowing black hair. Some were convinced to change the DNA in a new and, for them, exciting way."

"Sex with angels?" Raphael muttered, shaking his head.

"I'm afraid so."

Raphael snapped a look at Trudy, who immediately said, "It wouldn't have happened between you and me, Mr. Aronson. It was just a test." He looked at Tafari. "There wouldn't have been an offspring between me and Barry. I took precautions."

"You rearranged things again," Raphael said, returning his

attention to Dagobert.

"Actually, we didn't. We were content to wait and see what came of what we had already done. It was incredible. This is in your Bible, too. You should look it up. But, as I have told you, there are other entities out there than you and us. And they too aren't God. But you didn't know that. You thought they were."

"You said you decided to watch it," Raphael said. "Did you stay here, or could you see it from somewhere else?"

"We stayed here. This time, it wasn't just the genetic team. This time we were accompanied by military in case we needed protecting, and some others who were capable of all manner of what your ancestors called magic."

"Atlantis," Raphael deduced, then looked up and said it again as a question. "Atlantis?"

"Right. At the time, we were living on an island continent in the sea west of Europe, trying to stay out of touch with people. We sometimes also went to other inaccessible places like mountains or deep caves, the forests of Lesbos, but mostly we lived on what you called Atlantis."

The dark-haired Merovingian seemed to become lost in his own silent thoughts. Then he blurted, "Giants they were, the frightening offspring of the 'others' and women of Earth, tremendous human half-breed giants. They killed and ate everything—plants, animals, humans, each other. They had no souls. They had no conscience. We were studying them. They even had some of our magical powers. We tried to contradict that by teaching the human women we knew to cast magic and create weapons that could stop the giants. Inadvertently, we caused women to become feared by men, and they were subjugated, made to cover their faces and hair so as not to further entice the others. As to the giants, some died, some were killed, but some flourished, and we were beginning to deal with it when," He turned to face Raphael. "You ask about God and Jesus? We didn't even have to do anything. A huge flood wiped out the targeted population, most of what was left of the aberrant animals, and the crossbreeds and left mostly pure humans. Pure Homo-Sapiens. The ones who survived were called Noah. We thanked God and went on with our existence. That flood, however, was the end of the foreign seed in the farmer's soil. Or so we all thought." He turned and looked meaningfully at the women.

"Right," said Raphael. "I know. It's in the Bible, but we didn't pay attention."

"Right. But it left those we had engineered. They were still there in the group that was saved. Still, even though the Neanderthals were now extinct, there were still the genes of both Neanderthal and Homo-Sapien in human beings, and we now believe, looking at your Entitleds group, there was left some of the, how do you call it, bad seed from the days of giants. And they both were endowed now, through interbreeding, with the FoxP2 gene, and they also retained some of the genetics of the Fallen Ones. This is what your religious people have long called the punishment for original sin."

"Oh God," Raphael said. "Eve wasn't at fault for the new humans after all. You were. Hold on. This is all getting very confusing. From what you are saying, 40,000 years ago your people starved out the Neanderthals and tried unsuccessfully to do the same to the Denisovans?"

"I'm afraid that is correct," Dagobert said.

Raphael knew he had heard some of this story before, possibly in his own bible. "But the humans who were left had Neanderthal genes and the genes of some evil god, and on top of that, the genes of some other, what were they, some other entity? All the different forms of humans began to wage wars on each other and were killing and eating each other?"

"Not all," Dagobert corrected, "or we would have ended it there. We decided to stay here and help. It was the least we could do. It was what we would have wanted humans to do for us if the roles were reversed. We were doing fine with humans, but the entity, the fallen angels, were gaining ground?"

Dagobert nodded. "Then there was the flood from the Bible?"

"Not just the Bible but from many other religious and history books," Trudy added.

Raphael peered at them for nearly a full minute before assessing, "There was a flood, but it didn't work, and our genetics were still all screwed up? We still were not basically good."

"Right."

"Holy shit, why didn't you go home and leave us alone?

Couldn't you see that everything you did made it worse?"

"We couldn't just leave. We had caused the problem. And this is our home, too."

"So, then you found out we were still screwed up, and, of course, you added another mutation to our genetics? What are you people, stupid?"

"Actually, it was two mutations. We kind of had to. From the animal Neanderthal DNA now in Homo-Sapien, and from the slight genetic change from interbreeding with foreigners, came the new humans. These new ones had an affinity to kill and eat what they killed, even each other, a predilection to vicious evil, and the worst part of all was that these new people still had the ability to choose whichever side they wanted, free will. Now they were using their free will for purposes other than what it was intended for. You were supposed to choose good; basically, be good, not basically equal parts of good and evil. You were supposed to begin at about eight days after birth to begin choosing one or the other, and evil, as it turned out, became your drug of choice."

"What was this FoxP2 gene? What is it supposed to do?"

"Your scientists called it the communication gene when they first found it, and that was pretty good. We were surprised they came to that almost perfect conclusion. It was for communications but not just language. The ultimate goal of the genetics is to make you more into the image and likeness of us, to enhance your spiritual side and lessen your material side. Tilt the scales in favor of good. Time, and therefore aging, is a correlation of spirit and matter. Matter wears out faster than spirit. You were supposed to live for a hundred and twenty years, but original sin had complicated that."

"But you said you don't die."

'I should have said we don't stay dead. We don't age in spirit. So, if you are more spirit than matter, you live longer. Pure spirit never dies. Pure matter has no soul and cannot be resurrected after death. That is why the offspring of the angels with humans left only spirit on the earth when they died. You call them demons. When you say, 'The good die young,' you couldn't be more wrong."

Morgan Baez had been silent for so long. Raphael thought she must be taking this in, as he was, and he wondered what she was believing or not believing, and perhaps what she already had known before this trip to fantasy land. He looked at her across the table, and she smiled.

"You said in the beginning you changed the DNA of some other animals and birds. How did that turn out?" Raphael asked his host while still looking at Morgan.

Tafari interjected, "Funny you should ask…" but Dagobert spoke over her after shooting a heated glance at his daughter. "Not well," he said. "Animals and birds, it seems, cannot contain spirit, only humans can. The next piece to make you into the image and likeness of us, so to speak, was to enable you to communicate nonverbally with each other and with us through what you called prayer. It is also designed to dampen your free will and absolve you from original sin. Human beings became thinking organisms. You became masters of abstract thought. No animals do that. No fully material beings can do that. Just you."

"Whoa, whoa, whoa, to dampen our free will? What are you talking about?"

"Yes. You will be able to work together finally, like a hive of bees, which was your destination from the beginning. To love God and treat each other the way you want to be treated. Everything was working well. Your books said the right things, your priests and leaders were doing what we wanted, culling the weak from the herd, moving directly to becoming our sheep. Then there was an abrupt turn in the road that we never foresaw."

"What now?" Raphael was entertaining a realization that these overseers of the world, these gods, might not be as benign or as intelligent as humans had given them credit for. "What didn't you foresee?" he asked.

"Jesus didn't agree with us."

Raphael sat back in his chair, and Dagobert did the same.

"Jesus is our God, too. He came to the underworld and told human beings they were being duped. This earth is, by the way, the underworld, not hell. Jesus pointed out to you that your leaders were wrong, and that they were teaching you the wrong things. He said they were 'like dogs who were sleeping with the cattle. The dog doesn't eat and keeps the cattle from eating too.' In essence, He told humans that they were worshiping an evil god, that the religious leaders didn't understand what they were supposed to teach, and they were teaching nonsense, such as blood sacrifices, that would lead you to become sheep. This, of course was what we wanted, but Jesus saw more in you and tried to save you. He made you *his* sheep, not ours. We never saw anything wrong with our plan for you. He did."

"Who is Jesus? Is he God?" Raphael asked.

"Our scriptures, and some of yours, explain it. He didn't begin in Bethlehem. After thought became real in the universe, the spirit we both call Jesus Christ was the first born. He was the first to be able to become spirit or matter rather than being restricted to one or the other. Along with his 'sister' Sophia, He became part of the trinity. The father, (the first thought), the son (Jesus), and the Holy Spirit (Sophia). Her name means wisdom."

Raphael now looked at Morgan. He wondered if she was accepting that this Sophia, the new character in this ongoing story, could possibly be real. When it appeared that she was, Raphael stood up from the table and began to pace along the side where his chair was. As he passed his empty seat, he laid a hand on it, almost for stability. It had occurred to him that if Dagobert was actually an angel, then Morgan couldn't be his cousin. So, who was she?

"And she is the one who screwed up?" he asked the angel sitting at the head of the table. "Sophia? Wisdom?" Without any proof, Raphael harbored more than a little skepticism.

"Sophia, as I have told you, in trying to create the first

god of Earth, made a mistake and Yaldabaoth became alive. He stood up, began his creation, and demanded that he be worshipped because he was, 'The Lord thy God, you shall not have gods before me.' Since Sophia created him, she and Jesus came to alter the course of the Earth. A second god was created, Sabaoth, and, with the help of the creator, He became a good God who defeated his predecessor but didn't kill him. Yaldabaoth could not die, so he continued to be the evil one who had already created everything, including a form of human being subjects who were both good and evil."

"You are saying human beings were created by an evil god?" Raphael was dumbfounded. This had never occurred to him as a possibility, but it answered a lot of questions, such as why God would tell Joshua and the Israelites to kill every man, woman, and child inside Jericho.

"Yes. You were created by an evil god, but you were ministered to by a good God. The two gods became one in your scriptures. In ours, they remained two."

"This is too much for me. I'm having trouble following it," Raphael said.

"Then you see why it was never told to you except in some ancient books where we tried and failed to explain it to humans. We gave up and decided to tell you only what we needed to make you follow us."

"And be your slaves. Who are you to do that? *We* have even stopped owning slaves."

"We are only the second formed, but we were before you."

"You are angels?"

"We don't call ourselves angels, but some do. Your potential was seen, and further experiments with DNA were forbidden around the time of Noah. The only thing we are allowed to do with humans is track the progress by periodically checking your DNA to see how far it has evolved. You must understand, we never wanted you to progress to a point where you could ascend to heaven and live amongst us or with God himself. That just was never the plan. The plan has always been that you are to progress to a point where we can live amongst you on a planet you haven't destroyed. You have to understand, Heaven wasn't ever supposed to be one singular place. This Earth is meant to be heaven as well. We were all meant to live here from the beginning.

"Jesus saw promise in you and called you His sheep and told you what you needed to know to allow you to fulfill the promise yourselves; to care for each other, to communicate with each other, and to communicate with Him through prayer. But you killed his material form. Just as our human forms have been killed many times. You still are driven by those aberrations in your genetics that make you want to wage wars, kill, and eat your enemies rather than love your enemies, or not care much about your neighbors at all. He tried to teach about spirit and matter, but few were listening, and even fewer understood."

Raphael was incensed for himself and embarrassed for humans. He knew Dagobert's assessment of human beings was accurate. That the instinct of these polluted beings saw their ultimate solution for everything was to kill those who disagreed with their religion, form of government, or way of life. Never in the history of the Earth had humans possessed the courage or the ability to live in peace.

"Tell me again, because I obviously wasn't listening either," he said.

"Time, and therefore aging and death, are a function of the correlation between spirit and matter. Matter wears out faster than spirit."

"But you said you don't stay dead, right?"

"That is true. The angels were born of spirit and are allowed to take on matter. Humans are the opposite. They were created from matter but gained the ability to grow spirit. Therefore, if you are more spirit than matter, you live longer proportionally. Pure spirit never dies. When we are total spirit, we do not even age. Jesus taught that if you, like the angels, grew in spirit, you would not stay dead either. If you grew to where you made good choices, positive choices, more often than evil or negative choices, you would fill yourselves with spirit and live forever. But no one listened."

"Resurrection?" Raphael's interest was prodded by his own knowledge of how Berga's story was being borne out by scripture.

"Yes. Now let's get back to who we are and what we have done. But first let's go outside. It is beautifully clear today, unlike the usual fogged-in harbor. The visibility is almost endless."

# Chapter Seventeen

*Jesus said, "Blessed is the lion which becomes man when consumed by man; and cursed is the man whom the lion consumes, and the lion becomes man."*
*– Gospel of Thomas, Nag Hammadi, Codex II*

*"What one man calls God, another calls the laws of physics."*
*– Nikola Tesla*

Trudy, Morgan, Dagobert, and Raphael walked outside the stone building into the natural beauty of the grass-covered mountaintop with nothing between them and Europe except an ocean separating the old and new worlds, and when the others were seated on the two benches facing the harbor, the host settled on a waist-high rock and continued.

"This last time we came, when I took this name as a Merovingian in Gaul, we studied and decided you were nearly ready to be finished. To be made ready to create the final stage of our planet. We have been working on your final change for the past fifteen hundred years. This is the end game. We are nearly there." He assessed Raphael's response.

"What if I intend to tell everyone about this silicon dioxide thing and the transmitters in the TVs and—"

He cut Raphael short. "Stop, stop, stop. What you have learned is of no use to you or anyone else. It didn't bother us that you all knew it. What's good for the goose is good for the gander," Berga said, "such a colorful saying. The quartz catalyst is obsolete. It was just meant to enhance the effects of the new genetics. We weren't allowed to change the genes again, so we helped the old genes change faster by themselves. The genetics were supposed to have been altered again in 2012, the end of the Mayan calendar. That wasn't their calendar, by the way. It was ours. We weren't allowed to by law, but now it is no longer needed. The catalyst pushed the genetics to where they must be. The FoxP2 gene now works fine and is in no need of any help or assistance. The communication gene is fully formed. You are nearly where you are supposed to be. We have only a few steps left to establish, and then we will stop broadcasting anything through the television. The Patriots test was meant to test how fast we could imbed an idea in the entire population of Earth. Everything is now fine."

"How can you say that? How can you say everything is fine? What about these damn incessant wars?"

Even as he was forming the question, Raphael heard a thought ringing in his head. "There are no wars."

"I need to show you something," Dagobert said, smiling at Morgan. He rose from his rock and motioned for the group to return to the house. Inside, he beckoned them to follow him into the room with the TV. He took a remote-control device from the shelf behind the television and turned on the TV, which was built into the wall. Then calmly said, "Watch."

In front of Raphael on the screen was the morning news, telling about the wars in Africa and Mexico. Apparently, the war with Mexico had been pushed back into Mexican territory and most of Africa was now liberated. Dagobert turned off the TV and said, "Your leaders had found that in order to keep the economies of all the nations going strong, we needed a robust military-industrial complex. We agree with that assessment. The world flourishes with the annual purchases of new weapons to replace those destroyed by war. The most confusing dilemma humans had recently was that to end war was to topple the economies of the world. There was only one thing to do." He switched the television back on, but with the push of a button, the screen showed something Raphael couldn't place. There was a desert which he assumed was in Africa until the camera, which appeared to Raphael to be floating over the landscape as if being carried by a drone, came across a trapezoidal wooden frame holding a large white sign in its middle. It said, "Death Valley National Park, home of the Timbiska Shoshone." The drone followed a blacktopped two-lane road with a double yellow line in the middle for a few seconds, then took a left and flew beyond the first mountainous hill of sand. There in the valley was a pile of rubble. As the drone flew closer, Raphael could see what it was. In a pile several times larger than the building where Raphael lived was a metallic mountain.

"Are those drones?" Raphael asked. There was no answer. He walked closer to the TV. The pile was in fact drones, and rifles, and airplanes, and rockets, and bombs, ammunition, and all types of military technology, and none of them seemed used at all. Aronson assumed there were also all the cars, trucks, and cell phones that had been destroyed.

He turned to Dagobert for an explanation.

"We decided we could have what we needed economically without wasting lives. Every day the weapons of war are driven or flown out to the desert and discarded. Then more are created and bought. It is a mutually accepted practice among the world's governments. Then, by lottery, land is transferred, and borders moved. And no one is killed." He turned to Raphael. "Were you ever drafted?"

"No."

"Do you know anyone who was drafted?"

"No, I just assumed."

"You assumed only the Entitled were drafted. They assumed the same about you. In truth, the only ones in the army are Associates who we know will not make known what is going on. There actually are no fighting armies except for show and to fly the planes and drones, and they volunteer. What soldiers you see on the televisions are computer generated. It has worked for generations. You just didn't know it. We are not evil. We truly are trying to get you to where you are supposed to go."

"What are you going to do with us? What are humans doing here? Where are we going?"

"Yes, those would be the right questions, now that you know where you came from. Well, I have told you my name. It is that of a Merovingian king. Trudy is my wife. The Merovingians last reigned in your 600s AD. The last king was Dagobert, me. I have not taken his name. It is my name. I am he. ReginTrude did not take the name of his queen. It is her name. The ring is real. The picture behind Tafari's wall hanging is of her father, me."

"However, if you even half believe me, you know I have been around a lot longer than fifteen hundred or sixteen hundred years. I have been called several things. I have been called nearly every name you have for god, from Yaweh to Jehovah, to Melchizedek, El Elyon, Elohim, Mohammed, Buddha, Vishnu. I have been called by every angel's name from Michael to Raphael to, well, every name you have heard and more. I have been called necromancer, druid, Atlantean, I have been called angel and devil, the offspring of Jesus and Mary Magdalene and the offspring of Lucifer. I have been called Shamash and Horus, I have been called an alien, a time traveler, a dimension hopper. None of them is right. I am just a geneticist who is not human. I did not balk at serving mankind when asked, although some others did. Yes, we are what you have for a long time called angels. Only we are capable of simultaneously becoming matter-based and spirit. We are not created in the same way you are, so our travel from here to where we live and back is not hindered by space, time, or material weaknesses as you are."

"Wait, if you aren't us, and you aren't God, and you aren't angels, who, or what, the hell are you?"

"Let me continue," Dagobert said, taking a few steps. He sat down next to Trudy and put his arm around her. "When we returned, about fifteen hundred years ago, and set up in France, we began the next to last phase of your evolution. We were called magicians, wizards, it was said that we had been born of a woman and a sea beast."

Trudy, Tafari, and Dagobert all laughed at the thought. "I guess in the beginning we did come from the sea that time. It was just that looking out at the sea from Gaul, no one knew there was land out there so they figured we must have come from the sea. We had once lived on that small continent that was destroyed in the planetary upheaval. We then spread out to a lot of different places. We were called the sons and daughters of angels, Tuatha de Danann, Nephilim, fallen angels, dragons, Merovingians, the anti-Christ, so many names and none of them true. Humans developed such imaginations! Some say we came from another dimension, or another time in the future, or even another planet. Pictures of us are on your cave walls, on your monuments of stone, but you decided it was safer if you saw them as the creative genius of cave dwellers and Egyptian kings. We didn't hide ourselves back then. We looked too different to meld with humans until your evolution took hold.

"It is hard to say who we are. We are from another place, and we are from here. We started out here millions of years ago but being of our makeup we weren't locked into Earth. As you have crossed lines between one species of human, an animal without a soul, to another species that not only has a soul but can pass it on to your children, we have crossed lines between angel and material. We are as different from you as you are from Homo-ergaster, more so even. Angels, for lack of a better name, do not age like humans, so here we are still. Let's just say we have been altering your DNA for hundreds of thousands of years so you can come to a place where you can live with us without destroying heaven.

"You realize you damn near destroyed the planet until we re-entered your society in the late twentieth century, and these incessant wars you were fighting. And, of course, nuclear weapons, and your insistence that the pollution you caused was not harming the planet. It's not your fault entirely, and we were trying our best all along to get you to fix the problem. It was the effect of original sin. We are just now getting close to fixing that. You know we have always found it strange that you never realized you weren't the ones responsible for original sin. You were the victims of it. But, Raphael Aronson, I am your friend. We are your friends."

"What do you think, Morgan?" Raphael turned to his longtime friend and boss. Morgan didn't answer but looked back to their host.

"Oh," Dagobert blurted, "there is another introduction you need to hear. Morgan is my closest Associate, my closest earthly friend. She brought you here. She befriended you for a reason. She is the one who suggested you in the first place."

"Now that that is out," Morgan said, turning to the young man guarding the entryway door, the one who had put a gun to her head in the first few minutes after Carlene's death to keep Raphael from attacking, "If you ever pull that nonsense again, put a gun to my head, it will turn out very unfortunate for you."

The boy smiled and nodded. "It worked. He likes you," he said sheepishly. Morgan Baez showed him a fist.

"No bickering," Dagobert admonished, also smiling. Then he turned back to Raphael and continued, "Tafari was to contact you, but she sometimes gets sidetracked. She has, however, given a good report of you, your caring and gentle ways, your deep concern for your friends, your acceptance of all levels of humanity. It seems you choose right over wrong much more often than not. My wife has also given you glowing accolades. It seems she tried everything she could to seduce you, even just coming out and asking you to sleep with her. She is quite beautiful, don't you think?" Raphael nodded. "You refused. Turned her down cold. She said you were a good Christian and would have none of a thirteen-year-old girl. I have to admit, I would have assumed you to like men, but Dumas put an end to that idea, as did my dear Associate. And you, Raphael, have been chosen."

Aronson looked around the group and realized he was the only one who was confused. "Chosen for what?" he asked.

"At the end of this year, the USR will win the final current war. It has already been decided. The government of the USR will become the government of the Worldwide Republic. And you are to be president of the Worldwide Republic. The economy will be kept afloat by a new fabricated hostile action against a fictitious otherworldly entity."

"Why should I do what you want me to do? Why should I give up free will for some sort of subjugated safety? Why would I believe all this, just because you say you're my friend?"

Dagobert answered, "Do you want to go ahead and destroy everything? Do you want to die off or live in hell? Or do you want to lead mankind to its destiny, living in peace for myriad years, living all alone on a restored planet?"

The chill breeze that blew off the ocean and swept up the cliff to where they were sitting had become a deterrent to understanding. Morgan was the first to hint that it was a problem. She stood from the bench and nodded to Dagobert, inclining her head toward the building.

"I agree," Trudy said and also stood up.

The women led the way up the stone stairs and into the building. The breakfast dishes had been removed and the white tablecloth was gone. The room now looked more like a place for a convention than a place to have breakfast. Instinctively, they all took the same seats they had had in the morning. After

Morgan poured herself another coffee from the kitchen and they had all become seated and comfortable, Raphael asked, "So why will we be alone on this planet?"

"I don't understand your question," Dagobert said. "Why alone?"

"We aren't ready to come to heaven yet, and it isn't completely ready for us. It will be in a thousand years after you humans are taught your destiny."

"That's insulting. We might save it all, you know. We might surprise you. Even by your own version of all this, there are still good seeds left in us."

"You weren't doing too well. You are part Neanderthal, after all. And other parts of you are just plain evil. Original sin wasn't actually your sin, you know. This has been the problem all along. You were told this. You were told how to fight the problems. You paid no attention."

Dagobert rose from his seat at the head of the table, placed his hands palms down on the thick dark wood in front of him, and looked directly at Raphael, who was also standing. Trudy sat to the right of Dagobert's chair and Tafari to the left. Morgan has become comfortable beside Trudy and Raphael's chair was next to Tafari. It was obvious that the angel wanted his newest friend to sit back down. He waited long enough for the women to all turn their attention to Raphael, who locked eyes in defiance with the host for a long few seconds and then he sat down. "Think of this," Dagobert began again. "The Renaissance the FoxP2 gene had evolved into what it was supposed to be, but it wasn't strong enough to function on its own. It was going to take another forty or fifty thousand years, and you humans weren't going to let that happen. We realized the earth wasn't going to last that long. The genetics were supposed to dull your sense of free will enough so you could truly communicate. So, we could communicate with you and convince you to do what we wanted. Earlier on, some people were answered when they prayed, and they received the answers and wrote them down. And you threw half of that away in the fourth century. There were the old and discarded books of the Jews and the books before that which were replaced with made-up stories written by those who would have you believe their nonsense. And there were the scriptures tossed out by those who compiled the current Bibles. There were the words of Paul, James, the Gospel of Truth, The Secret Book of John, of Thomas, Philip, Enoch, even Gilgamesh. Later, a few minds caught on. It is what saved you from being annihilated. People like Da Vinci, Tesla, Einstein, and some of your saints, the heads of some religions. Would you like a list of those we communicated with? Let's see, there were Socrates, Copernicus, Kepler, Galileo, Descartes, Pascal, Newton, Boyle, Faraday, Mendel, Kelvin, Plank, Einstein, Hawkings, Ramanujan, Von Braun, Berners-Lee, and more, but how many of those do you even know? The arts flourished because your free will was dimmed to allow for enough discipline to be created and for us to communicate your creativity, and because of that, you produced the great painters, architects, sculptors, musicians. We had hope for you again. We felt you would soon be able to communicate as a species."

Raphael was frustrated. "Communicate with who?"

"Good question. With your own self, with all the others, and with us. We left the idea of prayer with you, and you kept trying, but it wasn't working the way it was supposed to. You asked for stupid things, and when you didn't get what you had asked for, you dumped the whole idea. It was supposed to be a back-and-forth communication, not a lottery."

Dagobert turned to Tafari and Trudy. "Please God, can I win the sweepstakes." They laughed. "Prayer was to be your communication with us, but most of you weren't strong enough, and the genetics hadn't caught up.

"We hung around a while and began to enhance the genetics with silicon dioxide. It was also supposed to help with senility, the early decomposition of your minds, and it was supposed to allow for communications between humans and with us. Men were supposed to live a hundred and twenty years but were losing their minds at seventy because of the mixed genetics. We wanted you to grow to a place where you would not lose your minds so soon. The same with what you somewhat appropriately called the communication gene. You just weren't communicating. The genetics were weakened by your interbreeding and some other outside interference. Good seeds were losing the battle."

"Who decided that?" Raphael nearly shouted.

"You just didn't understand what you were supposed to be

doing. Treat others well? Believe in God? Thou shalt not kill, cheat, lie, steal. Ring a bell? Your own country had become enamored of the Republican Party for its racism, chauvinism, sexism, hatred of the poor, and its penchant for war and greed, so we stole their thunder and called our family the Republic. First, we altered the Supreme Court in the U.S. then bought the party through a SuperPAC, infiltrated the United Nations, caused regime changes in the Middle East, and rebuilt the Soviet Union and the United Kingdom and we unified South America. We allowed China to once again take over the entire Far East, and then just bought the whole damn thing with a massive amount of bribe money we stole from you through corrupt banks and bankers."

"But weren't they, the Republican Party, weren't they kind of against what Jesus said?"

"Yes, but we had given up on getting you to pay attention to doing things right. We decided to revert to the original goal for humanity."

"What was that?"

"Well, slavery, sort of. And to worship the almighty, which you thought was us. But now you have found out how we did that. It is true, we have made it so we can communicate the same things to all of you at the same time, and we could, by means of your wireless technology on televisions, implant in you a set of rules that you would accept without question since your free will had been compromised. We used technology to fill in the gaps in what was supposed to be natural. And now that it is about to become natural, you want to run out and tell the world."

"I do," Raphael Aronson said. "You have no right to take our God-given free will. I will stop you. We will stop you."

"No, you won't." Dagobert smiled like a cat and stretched his arms behind his head. "You might have stopped us if you had paid better attention, but you didn't. Now you are destined to do what you are told and make this planet livable. But if you want, you can go out and tell everyone what you know. It has happened before. Some will believe you and be laughed at. Some won't and will do the laughing. Jesus told you through messengers and then even came here Himself and told you, and how did you listen to him? You killed his corporeal body. You are supposed to work together, to care for one another as if you are one. But since you won't do it of your own volition, we are going to make you do it.

"It doesn't matter. Tell who you want. Within a few generations, your evolution will be complete. You will be in total communication with our thoughts, and you will communicate them to each other, and the human race will become what it was always supposed to be. A singular entity. There isn't going to be a big fight. You've already lost."

"So, we are supposed to become like an ant colony?"

"Better. More like bees. You were given free will. It became poisoned beyond repair. We intend to take it away. And you have found out too late. It is inevitable now. Have you ever watched a hive of bees work together without any verbal communication? This is what you will become. You will work together to create a world as perfect as is possible, given what you have already maimed forever. You will care about each other as you care about yourselves. Eve was told, 'You will be like the Gods if you eat this.' They never ate it, Raphael. We implanted it and fed it, and changed it, and enhanced it. It was a lie, but a necessary lie."

Raphael's attention was taken by a fly caught inside the window directly behind Dagobert. It was obviously looking out at a world that called to it beyond the glass pane. No matter how hard it tried, the pane kept it from breaking free and enjoying the sunshine and freedom of the outer world. Again and again, it flew headfirst into the glass, buzzed, retreated, and tried again. Dagobert saw what was stealing the man's attention and went slowly to the window. With a swift swipe of his hand, he caught the fly and held it in his hand. He turned back to the table and looked directly at Raphael. The angel whispered into his hand and let the fly go. Raphael watched it dart from the window and across the room to the open door and out into the sunlight. Dagobert smiled and sat down. "So, you are the devil, the serpent?" Raphael asked after a few seconds.

"Don't worry, Raphael, we are not the devil," Dagobert said. "You are closer to being the devil than we are. We introduced an existing entity to the power of verbal and non-verbal communication and the power of abstract thought. You were even unknowingly given the ability to understand each other's thoughts. And you were given the ability to choose good or evil. You were created from evil. That is not our fault. You had the evil in you from before we arrived."

Dagobert leaned forward as he made his point. His mannerisms were relaxed, which insulted Raphael. This was humanity's future they were discussing, but this… person/angel acted like it was nothing. "We left some of our people here to watch over you," he continued. "We have always been watching you for a million years around the planet. We became the exalted ones in Rome, Greece, Africa, South America, Europe in the new continents, pretty much everywhere. In your ignorance, there were even some humans and otherwise entities who were not us who became your gods. That set things back into millenniums of darkness. Then a new move brought us to what is now called France. We ruled there for a while then got tired of it and decided to speed up the evolution of the genetics we had installed, and we coddled our newest version of you. The silicon dioxide is like a battery, and it worked fine to enhance the effects of the old genetics. Now the gene is working by itself, although it is in its infancy. We don't need televisions or electrical impulses from silicon dioxide. We can communicate directly all at once. Well, in a few decades it will be finally possible."

He smiled, the expression chilling to Raphael. "You will be like bees or dung beetles. That is all you are, you know. You are not gods. You are not even angels. Damn, you're not even what humans are supposed to have been. Pretty much, given the choices you made, you are livestock. But you are livestock who have created a soul and have become capable of giving that soul to your offspring. That is your only real accomplishment. That is what made you special. We can't do that, but then again, we don't have to because we don't die or multiply in our spirit form.

"This is why we took bees as our symbol, in many cases. What we have done dampens free will, allows us to control those who would not normally be controlled, were not created to be controlled."

Raphael took a sip of his water, his thoughts swirling. There had to be a way to stop this insanity.

As if he knew what Raphael was thinking, Dagobert sat back down and said, "Do you understand how much energy you have in your puny body? Do you realize how much spirit can be contained in matter? How about it? Do you realize how much spirit can be created by matter?"

Raphael squinted and stared at his host. "No. I don't," he said to Dagobert's obvious arrogance.

"You of course know of Albert Einstein, and you of course know the equation, $E=mc^2$?"

Raphael nodded, knowing this wasn't the end of the question. "Relativity," he said.

"Seems simple, doesn't it? And I'm sure you think no one has ever told you how much matter creates energy and how much energy it takes to create matter. If you understood this, you would understand what you lowly humans have done to be called 'a marvel of marvels' by God himself, and He did call you a marvel in the scriptures."

Dagobert held up a book and recited from memory.

*Jesus said, 'If the flesh came into being because of spirit, that is a marvel.*

"That is us," Dagobert said, then glanced at the book again.

*'but if spirit came into being because of the body, that is a marvel of marvels.*

"That is you," he added.

*'Yet I marvel at how this great wealth has come to dwell in this poverty.*

"That is the problem," Dagobert finished. "That is from the Gospel of Thomas. You claim your honest ignorance of this, but several people have explained this to humankind over the years. I have to admit that most of those people didn't explain it so you could understand it, or if it was understandable, it was hidden. This has been a problem all along; a few intelligent people understand something, and they tell all the others who are not so intelligent and do not understand it, and the world still only has a few intelligent people who understand what is truth." As he reached into his boot and pulled out a tattered printout of what appeared to be some type of article, Dagobert explained, "A young man, however, named Joshua Carroll, a student of the stars, told you in 2014 exactly what you need to know in a manner that was quite understandable.

"This," he said waving the quarter-folded copy paper in the air, "is his explanation in an article he wrote for an internet blog called *Universe Today* back in 2014. He said this equation 'represents the correlation of energy to matter... Many people are unaware of just how much energy is contained within matter... I will attempt to convey to you the magnitude of your own personal potential energy equivalence.'

"The measure of energy," Dagobert explained, "is the equivalent of the measure of spirit. Positive and negative together; good and evil. Do you understand what I'm saying? We can measure the spirit of a human being by measuring his or her energy. Is that understood before we go on?"

Raphael nodded, tired of Dagobert's attitude. "I get it. I'm not stupid. What is not matter is spirit. What is not spirit is matter."

"Okay, then understand that your choices fill up either side; good or evil, positive or negative.

"As Carroll put it when he was just an undergraduate:

"'E represents the energy, which we measure in Joules ... All this essentially means is that a Joule of energy is equal to the force used to move a specific object one meter in the same direction as the force.

"'M represents the mass of the specified object. We measure mass in kilograms.

"'C represents the speed of light... or rather 300,000,000 meters per second. So essentially what the equation is saying is that for a specific amount of mass (in kilograms), if you multiply it by the speed of light squared $(3.00 \times 10^8)^2$, you get its energy equivalence (Joules).'"

Dagobert looked at Raphael, hoping to see understanding in his eyes. "Energy and spirit are measured the same." He saw the understanding, so he continued. "Carroll goes on to say he is going to show an experiment that 'isn't intricate and doesn't need any fancy equipment.' He also explains in his article that he is using the equation 'in its most basic form.'"

Dagobert took a moment to assess Raphael's size. "I would say, Raphael, that you weigh about 190 pounds?"

"About," Raphael answered.

"Well, that is perfect, since Carroll's experiment used 190 pounds also, his own weight at the time. To show you how much energy you humans have within your tiny bodies, this has to be converted into kilograms. Do you know the conversion rate?"

"No," Raphael said with a smirk, knowing Dagobert was playing with him.

"Here it is:

"1 human = 190 pounds

1 pound = 453.6 grams

So, 190 × 453.6g/1 = 86,184

One human your size equals 86.18 kilograms.

"Are you following along with Carroll's experiment?"

Raphael nodded. It was, so far, fairly simple.

"Now we can plug the values into the equation and see just what we get:

$E=mc^2$

$E= (86.18kg)(3.00 \times 10^8 m/s)^2$

$E= 7.76 \times 10^{18} J$

"As in Carroll's experiment, that is 7,760,000,000,000,000,000 or roughly 7.8 septillion Joules of energy.'"

"You know," Raphael said, shaking his head, "that means so fucking little to me, it could be in Greek. Why do you think it is so well explained?"

"Just remember that the amount of energy in a human is that huge number. The experiment didn't finish here. He went on to say this enormous amount of energy still seemed 'vague,' and he added, 'What does that number mean? How much energy is that really? Well, let's continue this experiment and find something that we can measure this against to help put this amount of energy into perspective for us. First, let's convert our energy into an equivalent measurement. Something we can relate to. How does TNT sound? First, we must identify a common unit of measurement for TNT. Now we find out just how many kilotons of TNT are in one Joule.

"Carroll went on to prove that one Joule of energy is equal to .000000000000239 kilotons of TNT. That is a very small number. A better way to understand this relationship is to flip that ratio around to see how many Joules of energy are in one kiloton of TNT. One kiloton of TNT equals $4.18{\times}10^{12}$ Joules, or rather 4,184,000,000,000 Joules."

Dagobert noticed that Raphael's head hung, sagging as if to eject the webs of confusion that had been spun by the equation. "You don't have to understand that equation, just remember the two numbers. One kiloton of TNT equals 4,184,000,000,000 Joules; One human equals 7,760,000,000,000,000,000 Joules," the Merovingian said.

"Big difference," Raphael answered.

"Let me read you what Carroll's article said next. Something I'm sure you will understand '…one human being is roughly the equivalence of 1.86 MILLION kilotons of TNT worth of energy. Let's now put that into perspective, just to illuminate the massive amount of power that this equivalence really is.

"The bomb that destroyed Nagasaki in Japan during World War II was devastating. It leveled a city in seconds and brought the War in the Pacific to a close. That bomb was approximately 21 kilotons of explosives. So that means that… one human being, (has) 88,403 times more explosive energy… than a bomb that destroyed an entire city… and that goes for every human being.'"

Dagobert folded up the article and slipped it back into his boot. He waited for Raphael to look at him, but before he could say another word, Raphael spoke up. "Energy is spirit. There is positive and negative energy. There is good and bad spirit. Positive energy produces more goodness; negative energy produces bad, and vice versa. There is a certain total amount of energy in each human being, but our free will controls if there is more positive or negative, good or evil. And this is written in Einstein's Theory of Relativity?"

"Bravo!" Dagobert shouted, leaping to his feet. "Bravo, Raphael! Now think of what would happen if all humans were subliminally communicating that to each other, the negative or positive, the good or evil, and each human was affected by each and all the others. Think of what would happen to the world. Evil would grow and be passed on, one to another."

While Raphael was still thinking about the seesaw effect that might occur, Dagobert leaned forward and said in a lower, more intimate voice, "You humans have been choosing negative for quite a while—choosing self-aggrandizing over helping those in need of help, choosing war over peace, money over goodness, doing bad over doing good, filling your coffers over filling your hearts."

Raphael looked up and said meekly, "And now you are going to tell me it is also in our scriptures, and we haven't been paying attention."

Dagobert smiled. "Let me give you another quote from your own Bible. '…for whatever a man sows, this he will also reap. For the one who sows to his own flesh will from the flesh reap corruption, but the one who sows to the Spirit will from the Spirit reap eternal life. Let us not lose heart in doing good, for in due time we will reap if we do not grow weary.' That of course is from Galatians 6:7-9. Interpret it how you might, but if you feed matter, you will increase your matter. If you feed your spirit, you will increase your spirit. If you feed good, you will reap good; if you feed evil that is what you will reap. It is truth."

# Chapter Eighteen

*"The energy of the mind is the essence of life."*

*- Aristotle*

*"There are three classes of people: those who see. Those who see
when they are shown. Those who do not see."*
*- Leonardo da Vinci*

Raphael looked blankly off into the expanse of history.
"Damn," he said in final exasperation. "Isn't there
anything good we've done?"

"You are a marvel!" Dagobert exclaimed in honest
admiration. "You created your own souls. Even God was
impressed." The host waited a few minutes as if in his own
recollection of mankind and then asked, "Is there anything
else I can help you with, Mr. Aronson?"

Raphael paused. There had been other questions prior to

the answers he hadn't expected. One came back. "Why the three classes, if we are all so pathetic?" Raphael was noticeably upset. "Why have you splintered us? What are you afraid of?" Aronson felt a wave of fear pass over him like a wind from the ocean.

"The Entitleds are genetically weak willed, stunted, dumb, and were easily controlled by sports, war, beer, sex, lottery tickets, the pleasure of being chauvinistic and ready to kill for their country, of course their pleasure is more in the killing than their country. And they are filled with anger toward anyone who lives a better life, and that is pretty much everyone else. They were those who created what they believed were subcultures just to make themselves feel better to have someone beneath them. Their anger is controlled by the dampened free will. They just plain don't feel like doing anything that takes thought or energy and doesn't give them pleasure. Because they feel unarmed in any real intellectual conversation or argument, they live in little enclaves of like-minded people. There are weaknesses in their genetics, and they produce offspring just like themselves, but they are useful to us. And we don't even have to waste time on them. They are the ones who allowed us to take over the world governments. They will do what they are told, with or without genetic manipulations. They are pretty much the offspring of the Fallen Ones, only smaller and not as smart. Strangely enough, we told them to be Christian so they believe they are even as they break every law of Christianity.

"Then there are the Members. The Members are you who believe in the process we have endowed you with. Those who believe they have created the process in your own minds. The Members see the Entitled as lower class, although they are magnanimous enough to not say it out loud. And you see the Associates as your superiors, again, something you don't admit out loud. You help make things work and are closer to what you were supposed to have been in the first place, and if you aren't, at least you are capable of producing children who can be convinced. But there are flaws in your decision making, especially when it comes to good versus evil. You seem to know which side of a decision is good, but you just don't seem to have the courage to choose it on a consistent basis. You do just as much evil as the Entitleds, but you hide it or deny it to others, and they accept your lies because they are themselves hiding the same things. Ironically, you are outraged when you see the same characteristics in anyone else. The Members are those who are willing to work from within the system, together, and make things work better. They are truly a middle class, and they are physically afraid of the Entitleds, so they don't mind that their 'lower-class' brethren are oppressed.

"The Associates have been told everything, and they have listened and understood. They know from birth what they are supposed to be. They understand the inevitability of the end product of humanity. They are my brothers and sisters. They are your saints. Modern-day saints, and modern-day giants. They believe they are their brothers' keepers, that they are to treat others the way they wish to be treated. They are willing to take sustenance from one group to make sure the other groups are taken care of. They believe they are to love and serve in all things. They are seen by the others as traitors to their own people. And, sorry my dear friend," he looked sadly at Morgan, "but that is pretty much what they are."

He turned back to Raphael. "This was explained to you by an Egyptian poet Valentinius a hundred years before Jesus arrived. He said in his Gospel of Truth, 'There are those who are born and understand who they are and how they are supposed to act. There are those who have no remembrance of who they are supposed to be but still produce those who can be converted. Then there are those who have no remembrance at all and produce those like themselves who are driven by fear and despair, oblivion, confusion, and ignorance.' The first are the Associates, the middle are you, the Members, and the last are the Entitleds. It was also explained more precisely by da Vinci when he said, 'There are three classes of people: those who see. Those who see when they are shown. Those who do not see.'"

"And you?" Raphael had hidden his face in both hands and looked up for a moment.

"We are the Republic. We have made you special. You believe in God, albeit you believe in the wrong one. You believe all by yourselves that working together to a common goal is holy. You believe that to work apart is destructive. You don't have to be manipulated, or you won't have to be in a few hundred years or even as a few decades. You just need to be told what to do. It won't be like handing you a list of commandments from a god you never understood. The list will be your own thoughts. You will feel the thought being born in your heads and you will follow it because it will be of your own making. You have become your own warders, you built your own walls, your own chains, and now you love being incarcerated here in your filthy cities. There was a brief moment in the early 1970s when you as a people stood up and railed against the oppression of your own race of people. Then the voices were extinguished in the laughter and shouting of the Entitleds; the very ones you were trying to help. Now you will become what you were supposed to become, and we didn't have to do much. You were so willing to learn our rules and follow our lead, and now you believe you lead yourselves.

"And I am the Republic, and I too am more than one person. Today I am three. There are more, but they aren't here. They don't need to be here.

"Yes, we have come to the conclusion that you cannot be trusted with free will any longer." Dagobert seemed almost sad as he looked out over the precipice that dove to the ocean below. He turned back toward Raphael. "Did you know that the first Raphael was the angel who bound Azazyel and imprisoned him on Earth? Do you even know who Azazyel is?"

Raphael only looked with inquisition at the now bigger than life entity on the other side of the conversation. "I didn't know that. No, I don't know who Azazyel is," he said, feeling his own inferiority.

"But for a short time," Dagobert continued with near excitement, "we sat at the rail as if this were a horse race, and we cheered you on. If pride were not the downfall of every entity that has experienced it, we would have been proud of the combined creation of us and God.

"During your Renaissance, you brought out every form of art you could muster and displayed your inner beauty on canvas, and in literature, and in sculpture, and in religion. You went fearlessly into the darkness of ignorance and plucked out of it the courage to face the monsters of war, bigotry, chauvinism, hatred, fear, anger, selfishness, and greed. A few hundred years later, as we watched, humans as a group, either verbally or nonverbally, said 'Make love not war.' You can imagine how we felt when human beings grouped together and forced the governments to stop a war against the wishes of the evil ones. It was a powerful statement. And you pushed blindly into equality for everyone under your laws. For a time, the inhabitants of Earth had begun to realize you were all ancestors of two interestingly black humans who had lived in Africa. You even called them, 'scientific Adam and scientific Eve.'"

Dagobert leaned down and picked up a rock, then tossed it over the edge and watched it descend the cliff and fall into the harbor. "For a while, most of you stood up for what was right and just and good without wanting anything in return for it. Because black men of all ages were called by some 'boy' you began to call everyone 'man.' That was seen as a particularly satisfying act of intelligence to those who created you; especially because you had for a century been looking down on the race from which you had come. It had been the epitome of ignorance for you to believe that the race you descended from was inferior to you because of its race. For a while, intelligence was revered not feared. For a while, you cared what happened to others and even freely gave to those who had too little without labeling them lazy or stupid. For a while, we watched in awe as one country even welcomed those who were downtrodden and needed a place to be. But after the crest of the wave of enlightened humanity crashed in the rocks of greed and selfishness of the late 1900s and making and keeping your money became the reason for the existence of the majority of people, we began to lose faith in you. Then barely into the new millennium, fear, anger, and ignorance rebounded voraciously and devoured all that had been good in our experiment and threatened to destroy the whole planet with deadly ecological practices, horrific weapons, prolific wars, and a fragmenting of the people that had never been seen before in a million years.

"It was then decided that you would be allowed to continue, but since your free will had chosen evil over good, we would take away your free will. As a species you had your chance; now it is over. There will be a thousand years of peace while you rebuild paradise, and then we will decide what to do with you. Would you like to bring peace to your people Raphael?"

"I don't know. I have to think. I don't know how much of this I believe. Is there proof?" Raphael stood up so that he might look down on Dagobert, "What if I explain this all to the people, lead them in a different direction?"

"They won't go. Don't worry; this phase is going to take a little while. What you can do is make them comfortable being what they are supposed to become."

"And what is that exactly?"

"Builders, workers, drones, and queens, humans."

"Slaves," Raphael added angrily.

"If you wish," his host admitted.

"What if I won't do it?"

Dagobert turned and quickly dove from the cliff and plummeted four hundred and seventy feet toward the ocean below, and within an instant he continued his explanation from behind Raphael who turned to see the proof he had wanted.

Dagobert stood dripping wet on the hill behind him. "We hope you will, Raphael. You were chosen by your friend. Vetted by my own family. I believe you are who we need. You are a good person, an enlightened and caring human being, strong, not temptable, and you have asked all the right questions in life. We believe you do not fit into one of the three types. We believe you are someone who has known since your birth exactly who you are supposed to be, and you want your people to become more than they are. The small percentage of humans who believe as you do, act as you do, are the reason you are not being exterminated entirely. We expect you would want to lead them into a thousand years of peace and prosperity."

Raphael, stunned by the proof he could no longer deny, thought for a few seconds. "I'll do it. I'll be your president." He said in feigned resignation. He turned, had a thought, then stifled it and walked back inside to pack his bag. He proceeded back through the library and out into the garden where he sat down on a stone bench and quietly, contemplatively, looked off at the ocean. It was five in the morning, and Raphael waited for his car to arrive. The breeze from the ocean seemed to cool him one cell at a time, but it didn't matter if it was warm or cool. He sat perfectly comfortable on his rock.

"Do you think he believes us?" Dagobert asked of his wife and daughter.

"Does it matter?" Trudy answered.

"Have they ever?" added Tafari.

"Do you think he knows what he's getting into?" Morgan asked her friends as they began to follow Raphael through the ancient building and out the other side to face the wind from the ocean. Dagobert stopped just inside the door and told Morgan, "I doubt it. They never have paid attention to the fine print."

## About the Author

**John T. Hourihan Jr.,** a retired journalist, has won state, regional and national awards for his opinion column in several New England newspapers. He received the Cross of Gallantry for valor in Vietnam, where he served three tours as a Vietnamese linguist. He is disabled now from the effects of Agent Orange.

He lives with his author wife Lin Hourihan (*The Virtue of Virtues, The Mystery of the Sturbridge Keys*) in the woods of central Massachusetts. His other works include the Baltimore Catechism series: *Baltimore Catechism: The Fall and Rise of a Catholic Boy; Baltimore Catechism: Year of Confirmation; Baltimore Catechism: Mass of the Faithful; Baltimore Catechism: Sacrament of Reconciliation* as well as *The Eighth Commandment, The Mustard Seed – 2095, The Mustard Seed – 2110,* The Mustard Seed – 2130, *Beyond the Fence: Converging Memoirs, Parables for a New Age* I and II, and *Play Fair and Win*.

www.ingramcontent.com/pod-product-compliance
Lightning Source LLC
Chambersburg PA
CBHW011224190726
48287CB00008B/2735